The Space Between Before and After

THE SPACE BETWEEN BEFORE AND AFTER

Sue Stauffacher

Margaret Ferguson Books

Holiday House • New York

Margaret Ferguson Books

Copyright © 2019 by Sue Stauffacher

All Rights Reserved

HOLIDAY HOUSE is registered in the U.S. Patent and Trademark Office.

Printed and bound in January 2019 at Maple Press, York, PA, USA.

www.holidayhouse.com

First Edition

10 9 8 7 6 5 4 3 2 1

Library of Congress Cataloging-in-Publication Data

Names: Stauffacher, Sue, 1961– author.

Title: The space between before and after / Sue Stauffacher.

Description: First edition. | New York : Holiday House, [2019] | "Margaret
  Ferguson Books." | Summary: "When 10-year-old Thomas's mother,
  who suffers from depression, disappears, he creates a fantasy narrative in
  which his mother is safe and sets in motion a path of healing, not just for
  himself, but for his father and aunt as well"—Provided by publisher.

Identifiers: LCCN 2018005863 | ISBN 9780823441488 (hardcover)

Subjects: | CYAC: Depression, Mental—Fiction. | Missing persons—Fiction. |
  Family life—Fiction. | Storytelling—Fiction. | Healing—Fiction.

Classification: LCC PZ7.S8055 Sp 2019 | DDC [Fic]—dc23 LC record
  available at https://lccn.loc.gov/2018005863

To those with a beloved family member who suffers from depression,
may you find comfort in knowing you are not alone

The Space Between Before and After

Chapter 1

It was early December when Thomas came downstairs to get his breakfast and found his mother sitting at the kitchen table.

"I had the strangest dream last night," she said, looking up from her teacup, the one with the bluebells on it. She had a whole collection of flowered teacups.

Thomas froze. Not only was his mother awake, she was starting a conversation.

"What was strange about it?" he asked, wondering if he should continue to get a cereal bowl out of the cupboard or if he should stay where he was.

"I was in the airport. I must have been going on a trip." Helen stirred her tea with her spoon. The murmury sound of her voice made Thomas wonder if she was still there—in her dream.

Should I ask where she was going? Or wait for her to say more?

"I stood in the middle of the terminal, looking down the hall at all the gates."

Another long silence followed.

Should I get the bowl?

Thomas decided it wasn't time to move yet.

"Where were you going?" he finally asked, unable to hold on to the question any longer. This was, by far, the most interesting and longest conversation he and his mother had had in weeks.

Helen put her spoon down and said, "There was a ticket in my purse—but it didn't have a destination on it."

She flicked a toast crumb from her blouse and Thomas noticed something else. His mother had never worn that blouse before. It was a birthday present from her sister, his aunt Sadie; Helen's birthday was so long ago, it was almost time for it to come again. And the toast crumb had to be added to the list of astonishments. She'd seen it was there and brushed it away.

"Though I did have a seat assignment."

The new blouse and the amount of words gave Thomas hope that maybe they were coming to the end of this particular blue mood of Helen's. Glancing at the clock, he willed the second hand into reverse. If his father came up from his basement office to check on Thomas's progress, she might stop talking.

Nice and slow, Thomas pulled out the kitchen chair and sat down.

Helen looked into Thomas's eyes and said, "If I did go on a trip . . . I would write to you."

"Promise?" was the word that came out of Thomas's mouth. He didn't know why. His mother never went on trips. It was all very strange.

She pressed on his knee so hard he could feel the pad of his foot against the linoleum. "Promise." Helen let go and, after a moment, Thomas got up from the table and opened the cupboard that contained the cereal bowls.

"It would be good for you to take a trip," he said. "You should get out more."

That was Aunt Sadie's line. What his aunt had said when she'd stopped over for a visit recently—Thomas had an impressive memory for past conversations—was: "I'd be tired, too, if I were you, Helen. You really should get out more. At least get some exercise. All you do is sit here in the kitchen and look out the window at the birdbath."

Aunt Sadie had then gone to stand by the window and stare out at the backyard to confirm that was all there was to see. "Which could use a good cleaning, by the way. I can't imagine birds like to drink from their own toilet."

"I sit on the front porch, sometimes, when the weather's nice."

"What? And keep tabs on the old lady across the street? I'm sure that's entertaining." Taking hold of Thomas's arm, Aunt Sadie pulled him to her side. "Is that Giselle from next door? What is she doing with a shovel in November?"

Thomas looked over the side fence. "It looks like she's about to dig a hole."

"Why would she want to do that?"

Thomas could see this interested his aunt. He shrugged. Giselle often got home from school before Thomas and ran out to get her mail just as he was coming up his driveway from the bus stop. She asked all sorts of questions that made Thomas uncomfortable, though he tried to answer her. He did not want to be rude.

Because of their conversations by the mailbox, Thomas knew that Giselle was concocting a plan to cheer his mother up; but he didn't want to mention this in front of her, so he didn't answer out loud. Instead he looked into Aunt Sadie's eyes and told her that way.

There was a whole language of looks that his father and Aunt Sadie and he had developed over the past couple of years.

Thomas didn't know if other families also had things they didn't say out loud and so had to replace words with stares or blinking or pressing their lips together. But with his gaze, and maybe a little bit of his eyebrows, he conveyed to Aunt Sadie that it was something to do with Helen, with her...mood. And though he could see that Aunt Sadie was having trouble making the connection, wondering why Giselle would even know about her sister's moods, she let it drop.

"She doesn't go to my school," Thomas had said to fill the space. "We talk sometimes at the mailbox about...things. She goes to the Montessori school. She and her mom moved in at the end of the summer."

"That's right," Aunt Sadie said. "Her mother told me it was something to do with being bullied. They moved so Giselle could be closer to her new school."

Thomas and Aunt Sadie had then sat down at the kitchen table on either side of Helen. As if they'd planned this ahead of time—like a play.

"All I know about Montessori schools is drawing letters in sand and pouring beans into a cup," Aunt Sadie said. "Learning through the senses, right? Isn't that what Montessori is all about? I can't imagine how they teach children her age. History, for example. How do you teach history to a twelve-year-old in Montessori?"

"Maybe they do reenactments, like on the History channel," Thomas said. "I saw a show once where they did a reenactment of the Civil War. There was so much smoke, the soldiers couldn't see who they were shooting."

And that's how it was—Thomas and Aunt Sadie, or Thomas and his father talking up a blue streak, talking around his mother, making conversation for three.

But this morning, it was just Thomas and Helen in the kitchen, and the conversation they'd started turned into a thread like the silvery-spun web string you see at the end of a piece of blown glass, which Thomas also knew about courtesy of the History channel.

That's when his mother said the most startling thing of all: "Maybe I *should* go on a trip."

At the same time, his father called up from his office to say that he hoped Thomas had eaten his cereal because the school bus would be arriving any minute.

And the thread connecting Thomas to his mother disappeared completely.

Thomas tried to think of something to revive it, but all he could see were the dust motes that settled on the edge of the bread board that sat on top of the microwave. He imagined they were flour or powdered sugar, which they might have been.

A long time ago.

Chapter 2
BEFORE

After Aunt Sadie left on that day she'd spotted Giselle with the shovel, Thomas went outside to get a closer look.

He wished he'd put on his coat. It was always cold in mid-November in Michigan, but the wind that day had made it feel Christmas-cold. Hugging himself, Thomas thought of the warm kitchen and his mother, then decided he'd rather be out here. For a few minutes anyway.

Giselle had on a purple puffy jacket and hat and a pair of snow pants under her skirt. Thomas thought she looked like a purple-quilted marshmallow trying to dig a hole.

"I told you the other day..." Thomas raised his voice to get Giselle to stop digging and look up at him. "My mom doesn't like dogs." Thomas didn't believe this. He'd only said it to make Giselle give up the idea.

"Thomas," Giselle said in an exasperated parent-teachery way. "Your mom will love Frenchy. *Quel chien adorable!* What an adorable dog! Everyone says so. I'm telling you, my plan is perfect."

"You can't *make* a dog run away," he told her, watching the steam from their breath twist together.

"Yes, you can." Giselle's pale cheeks were flushed red. "Well, I can," she corrected herself. "Using various behavioral techniques."

According to their mailbox conversations, Giselle planned to be a psychologist when she grew up. Her mother was a very good one with her own practice. Giselle was going to follow in her mother's footsteps.

"Don't look so worried, Thomas! It's only for a little while. And you have a fenced yard. Tomorrow, before school, I'll put Frenchy's favorite treats on your side of the fence and he will crawl into your yard using this tunnel I'm making—I'll block him from returning with our trash can lid. Your dad will be at work, you and I will go to school, and your mom will be the only one to see him running around, and then..."

Gazing up at the gray sky, Giselle continued to imagine how it would all go.

Even with the fence between them, Thomas could see quite clearly the long fringe that framed her brown eyes. No, they had green, too, Thomas noticed. Like a cat's eyes.

But a cat's face was serious; Giselle had a round face, and her mouth was never still. If she wasn't talking, which was rare, she was laughing or smiling or humming a tune or biting her lip. Taking her whole face into consideration, Thomas thought it safe to say that Giselle considered the world to be—more than 50 percent of the time at least—a laughing matter.

"Frenchy will cover her with kisses and she will carry him inside and give him something to eat and they'll snuggle." Giselle stuck her arm through the fence to grab Thomas's arm, but she couldn't catch hold with her mittens. "Did you know that just petting an animal releases oxytocin into your bloodstream? Those are the same feel-good hormones you get from hugging your friends or when a mother nurses her baby . . ."

Giselle's voice had trailed off. It seemed to Thomas that she'd released some feel-good hormones just thinking about her wonderful plan, but he hoped she wouldn't mention anything about babies to his mother.

Then Giselle said, "*Voilà! Raison d'être.* That means, 'reason to be.' She will have rescued poor lost little Frenchy and will feel better. Now, no more talking. I need to dig."

The problem with Giselle, his father would say, was that she *believed* in the outcomes she imagined when, in truth, she had no idea what would happen. It was very foolish to believe in things that did not exist, according to Thomas's father. Stick to what is known and observable. Always have proof.

Somehow Thomas knew that if he said this to Giselle, she would laugh.

Chapter 3
BEFORE

The next day, the day of Giselle's plan, Thomas saw her throw dog biscuits into his yard and Frenchy squeeze under the fence to get them. Thomas was on the way to the bus stop and his father had already left for work. It made him nervous—so much so it felt like he had butterflies in his stomach.

After lunch his teacher, Mrs. Evans, sat at her desk and said, "It's that time of day when you digest your lunches while I help you increase your knowledge of the world."

Stocking School had an open technology policy, so fifth graders were allowed to use electronic devices in pursuit of knowledge. But Mrs. Evans was "up to here" with students consulting sites on the computer instead of her, so she had started the Ask Mrs. Evans box.

This segment of the class was growing right along with Mrs. Evans, who was pregnant with her third child. Thomas suspected she was spending more time on "Ask Mrs. Evans" because she relished every opportunity to sit down and "take a load off," as she liked to say. He had checked his theory with his best friend, Martin Templeton, who consulted his daily diary and confirmed that in September the segments averaged seven minutes, but since Halloween they had exceeded fifteen.

Martin was fond of soccer and reading and board games, but he especially liked counting. Anything and everything.

Mrs. Evans always read the questions silently first to make sure they were appropriate for impressionable young minds. After squinting at the first question, she let it flutter into the wastebasket. "This question about the steps preceding fertilization of the human egg will have to wait for my long-term sub. We don't cover human reproduction until the end of the year."

She took her feet off her footstool and pushed her rolling chair to where she could see George Panagopoulos.

"What?" George looked around at his classmates.

"It would behoove students to remember that their handwriting is as distinctive as a fingerprint."

"But I wrote it with my left hand!"

"And I have a master's degree in education. Let's try again, shall we? All right, then," she said, holding up another slip of paper. "Why do people call that sensation you get in your stomach 'butterflies'?"

Thomas often asked questions about butterflies, and this one felt appropriate for today.

"Now, that's a good question." Mrs. Evans repositioned her feet on the stool and, clasping her hands, settled them over her belly. "Did you know that there are more nerve endings sending signals to your brain from your digestive organs than from your spinal column?"

"Is that why it hurts so much when you get punched in the gut?" George wondered aloud.

"What is the Ask Mrs. Evans rule, George?"

"Save the questions until the end of the lecture?"

"The lesson. Until the end of the lesson."

"Right." George put his head on his desk and closed his eyes. The whole class, including Mrs. Evans, waited to see if George would decide to snore, thus choosing to wait out the lesson at the student desk in the hallway outside the classroom. But apparently even George had some interest in this question, because he remained quiet.

"As I was saying, with so many nerve endings in the stomach, scientists have called it the second brain. Scientists used to think the brain was directing digestion, but in the last ten years they've discovered that ninety percent of the impulses are being sent to the brain. This perhaps explains why we say we have a 'gut feeling,' because the brain in our stomach is communicating with us. Up here." Mrs. Evans tapped her temple to avoid any confusion. "That fluttery sensation can feel like butterflies are flying around in our stomach, so we call it 'butterflies.' But actually, it's our second brain's response to the stress we feel when we're around someone we want to impress or have a crush on and we don't know what to say or . . . when we're nervous before a big test. And I suspect,

George, that the unpleasantness of being punched in the gut has as much to do with the stomach's proximity to the diaphragm as it has to do with nerve endings."

Mrs. Evans patted her belly, signaling that she was through with butterflies and moving on. "'What makes bread rise?'" she read aloud from the next slip of paper. Settling both feet on the ground, she leaned forward, putting her elbows on her desk. "It's a good thing I majored in science, isn't it?"

Chapter 4

When Thomas got home from school the day his mother had told him about her strange dream, he started his chores.

"There's a reason for the saying 'First things first,' Thomas," his father always said.

First Thomas brought in the mail. Then he removed any papers from his backpack that his parents needed to see. This wasn't for his father, who followed the school e-news bulletins carefully, but for Helen, who didn't like computers and rarely turned hers on.

Using a thumbtack, he pinned up an announcement for the revised date of the French Club popcorn sale and the winter drop-off directions to accommodate the loss of parking spaces to mounds of snow. Next, Thomas took an erasable marker and crossed off the date on the laminated calendar on the fridge.

It was Monday, December 2.

That's when he first began to wonder where his mother was.

But it wasn't his job to wonder where Helen was. It was his job to now complete his homework.

Helen's computer was an old desktop model and took forever to boot up, so while he waited Thomas thought he'd eat the bowl of cereal he didn't have time for that morning. He got out a bowl and opened the cupboard that held the cereal and crackers.

Where could she be?

Helen was usually in the kitchen. Though she might be in her bedroom sleeping. Should he go look for her? Before Thomas could decide to go upstairs, he heard the handle turn on the side door. It was his father coming home from his teaching job at the community college.

"Where's your mom?" he asked.

Thomas shrugged and turned to the keyboard, brushing q-w-e-r-t-y with the pad of his index finger.

"That's odd," continued his father. "She said she was going to try to run a few errands but would be back by the time you got home. Thomas, verbalize that shrug, please."

"I don't know. I . . . just got here."

Thomas's father picked up his mug and reached for the coffeepot.

That's when the second mystery presented itself.

"Who drank all the coffee?" he asked, holding up the pot, which was as clean as if it hadn't been used that day. Helen didn't drink coffee. She drank tea. Thomas looked for her tea-cup and saucer. They were washed and set on the drain board.

Thomas felt a prickling on the back of his neck. Usually there was a salad plate with toast crumbs on the table. And the mug was next to the tea bag that Helen set carefully on its foil wrapper after she'd steeped her tea. Rinsing her cup was his chore. It was *his* job to keep track of how much tea had been drunk and how much toast eaten. They had to keep watch because Helen was growing thin again.

All the same things were occurring to Thomas's father. He went over to the cupboard under the sink where they kept the garbage. Yanking it open, his father tilted the can so they could both see in. There it was—Dr. Chen's Fog Mountain tea. Aunt Sadie had bought the tea from an old high school boyfriend, Frank Navone, who believed that everything could be fixed by the right combination of tea leaves.

The tea contained an herb called hare's ear root that was supposed to help with Helen's mood. To Thomas, it smelled like dirty socks. He never mentioned this because his mother had to drink it and his father didn't like flights of fancy, as he called them. In addition to teaching freshman composition at the community college, Mr. Moran was a freelance copy editor. It was his job to correct the mistakes of authors who took matters of fact into their own hands and made assumptions about them, as well as to fix their bad grammar.

The pristine coffeepot and the cleared-away dishes heightened the sense that something about today was different. His mother's dream, the new blouse, her sudden interest in running errands and tidying up...

Thomas felt a grabbing sensation in his stomach. It was different from the one he'd asked Mrs. Evans about and that his mother called "butterflies." It also didn't feel like what Helen called butterfly kisses—when she'd tickle his cheeks with her eyelashes. This sensation was more like...George grabbing Thomas's shirt and pulling on it. Or the way his stomach felt when his father told his mother they had to go back to the doctor because "This medicine's not working, Helen. We need to try something else so you will feel better."

Maybe they were caterpillars—more than one, by the feel of it—crawling along the lining of his stomach.

"I'm going to try your mom," Thomas's father said, pulling his cell phone out of his pocket. "If I don't reach her, I'll call your aunt."

Chapter 5
BEFORE

The day Giselle had let Frenchy escape into their yard and Mrs. Evans had informed his class about the stomach having a "second brain," Thomas came home to find the small rug they used to wipe their feet thrown outside on the driveway. He stood there a moment, looking at it curled over on itself, registering that his second brain did not like what he saw.

Thomas always entered his house through the side door. Just inside, on the landing, his father had installed hooks for their coats and Thomas's backpack, and placed a plastic tray for boots underneath. From the landing you could go either up to the kitchen or down to his father's office.

Once Thomas had opened the door and stepped inside, he was attacked by the living floor mop known as Frenchy. Moaning, the dog threw himself at Thomas's legs. Was he happy or miserable, Thomas wondered, leaning over and trying to find some eyes in all that fur. What he discovered was a piece of twine attached to the dog's collar and the banister leading downstairs. Thomas undid the twine from the banister and he and Frenchy went upstairs into the kitchen.

There was Helen with her back to him, standing at the sink.

"What's going on?" he asked her.

She turned at the sound of his voice. "The Dovers' dog got into our backyard." Helen's eyes followed Frenchy as he scooted over the floor like he was on the trail of the biggest varmint ever.

"You have to take him back, Thomas, as soon as they come home. Your father left a message on their machine."

"You don't like having him here?"

"Oh, it was fine until he started lifting his leg...well..." Helen shut the door that led from the kitchen to the hall, closing Frenchy in. "He can't settle. It must be all the new smells."

Thomas sat on the floor and crossed his legs. "Here, Frenchy. Here, boy." Thomas called to the dog, but he was headed for the pantry. "What kind of dog is he?"

"A mutt, surely." Helen sat sideways on a kitchen chair, her chin perched on the chair back, watching the dog's progress. "I would say Frenchy is...a cross between a Pekingese and, maybe with his tracking obsession, a schnauzer?"

Just then Frenchy burrowed into Thomas's lap and lay there panting. Helen got down on the floor next to Thomas, adjusting her skirt and letting her long legs stretch out under the table. Sensing double the attention, Frenchy rearranged himself to sprawl over both their laps, his head in Helen's and his hindquarters with Thomas.

"Do you think he's hungry?" Helen asked Thomas.

As if in response, Frenchy began to lick her fingers. "He's really quite sweet," she said, rubbing the top of his head. They sat there in silence for some time, petting Frenchy top and bottom. Thomas remembered Giselle's comment about petting dogs and nursing babies, and he didn't know if he imagined it, but it seemed like something inside his mother relaxed. She was looking at the cupboard opposite almost as if it were a window, one with a view that pleased her.

And she was talking—quite a bit . . . for Helen.

It was on the tip of his tongue to ask her if she might like a dog when he heard his father's step on the stairs and the words "Helen, are they home yet?" And Giselle was opening the side door without knocking—all at the very same time.

She must have run straight into Mr. Moran, because the words that came out of her mouth were, *"Je suis vraiment désolée, Monsieur Moran.* I'm so sorry to bother you—"

At the sound of her voice, Frenchy did a squirmy roll off their laps and Thomas scrambled to his feet.

But Helen stayed where she was—her skirt hiked over one knee.

Giselle rushed up the steps, swooping Frenchy into her arms and bringing energy into the house.

And light.

That's how it felt to Thomas.

Sliding onto the floor beside Helen, Giselle put her flushed face up next to his mother's and exclaimed: "Merci, Madame Moran! Thank you! What might have happened to poor Frenchy had you not intervened?"

"Helen, get up," said Mr. Moran. "Let me help you." But when he held out his hand, it was like Helen didn't even see it; he had to bend down and take hers from her lap.

Giselle pretended to be busy with Frenchy, but Thomas saw her watching them—saw her making up her own mind about things.

"I would stay and chat, but...oh!" Suddenly Giselle's mouth was full of fur.

"Thomas." Mr. Moran touched the sleeve of his son's shirt, directing him to Giselle's side. "Help Giselle home. And next time, Giselle, I'd appreciate it if you used the front door."

More than anything, Mr. Moran wanted to restore order: to push Giselle out, make Helen a cup of tea, and sit her down at the kitchen table.

Thomas studied his mother's face; she now looked the way she did most days, like clouds were passing over the surface of her eyes, like clouds reflected in water. So he walked out after Giselle, choosing to remember his mother's expression only a few minutes before, when she'd sat petting the dog on her lap.

"This dog is too much!" Giselle said, handing over Frenchy and linking arms with Thomas.

Thomas had to concentrate to hold tight to Frenchy and

the twine. As they walked up to Giselle's house, she produced a key from her pocket.

"Don't let go," she warned Thomas. "I'll never catch him. *Il n'a pas de discipline*—he has no discipline. Come in!"

Thomas had never been inside the Dovers' house, had only glimpsed it when he and Martin trick-or-treated with Aunt Sadie through the neighborhood. Now, even on this gray day, Thomas walked into a room filled with sunshine—walls the color of butter, and red and pink pillows lined up on the bench where Giselle sat to take off her jacket and boots. He put Frenchy down.

"Good boy, Frenchy, *mission accomplie*," Giselle said. "Do you think he made your mother feel better, Thomas?"

Thomas shrugged and asked, "Why do you talk in French so much?"

Giselle tilted her head to look at him, then patted the bench beside her. Thomas didn't sit down; he wasn't planning to stay.

"Because it sounds beautiful to me," she said. "Don't you agree?"

He did. "It reminds me of a chef on a cooking DVD that my mother and I used to watch together. He speaks French."

Technically, Philippe Duprée spoke in English, but he had a French accent. Just watching the DVD, Thomas had felt transported on a river of words. Closing his eyes and listening to Philippe gave Thomas a shivery feeling on the back of his neck.

"Why don't you take off your coat," Giselle suggested.

"I better go home." Looking around, Thomas realized that he did not want to. The color was seeping into his skin here. It felt . . . cinnamon. No, it smelled cinnamon. Or maybe it made him feel the same way cinnamon did, which was to remind him of baking and other nice things.

"Why? Your dad knows where you are." Giselle took out her cell phone and called her mom to tell her she was home. Even though he hadn't taken off his coat or boots, Thomas followed her into the kitchen with Frenchy at his heels, the twine trailing behind him.

"You can free Frenchy while I make us some hot chocolate. Not the powdered kind. That is a crime. My recipe is from Café Angelina on the rue de Rivoli in Paris."

Thomas barely heard what Giselle said, he was so struck by the Dovers' kitchen, with its walls the rosy color of the sky when the sun was rising.

"Is this glass?" he asked Giselle, running his finger over the surface of the pale green counter.

"Yes, it's made from recycled glass."

"Won't it . . . break?"

"Thomas, you look so worried. Of course it won't break. Watch." Giselle smacked her pot onto the counter. "See?"

He did see that and a watery reflection of himself. For a moment, he thought he'd like to press his forehead against its coolness. The counter reminded him of the little bits of glass he collected on a vacation to the beach, the kind that had been polished by waves and sand.

Giselle picked up Frenchy and placed him on the countertop. "Time to free this dog."

It seemed wrong to Thomas to put the dog on the counter, but he located the twine and began to untie it.

"Your mom should drink this," Giselle said, getting a pan out of the cupboard. "It's comfort food. The secret ingredients are patience and time. Patience—as my mother would say—is in short supply around here." Giselle poured milk into the pan, unwrapped a bar of chocolate, broke pieces of it into the milk, put it on a burner, and turned on the flame. "But your mom has all the time in the world, doesn't she?"

Thomas ran his finger along the lip of green glass. Even his father would have to agree with that statement.

"Now. While we wait, I'm going to assess you."

"Assess me? Why?"

"Because children who live in households with parents who are depressed have *three times* the risk of becoming depressed themselves. Don't worry. It's easy. Sit down and I'll be right back."

Thomas didn't want to sit on the stool beneath the counter, the one Giselle patted, and be assessed. He thought he should go home and do his chores, but where had she gone? Could he just leave? With a dog on the counter and something on the stove?

Giselle returned with an oversize book before he could escape. She put Frenchy on the floor and perched on the stool next to Thomas. Opening the book titled *The BIG Book of Funny Things*, she said: "I'm warning you, they're not that funny; that's part of the test. Okay, here's one. 'Why did half a chicken cross the road?'"

Glancing at Giselle, Thomas could see that the dimples at the sides of her mouth had deepened, but she kept her lips pressed together to keep any sound from escaping.

"'To get to its other side,'" Giselle read. She looked at him expectantly. "Well?"

Thomas smiled at her. "It's kind of funny," he said.

Giselle flipped a page. "Okay, here's a better one. 'What did zero say to eight?'" When Thomas didn't answer, Giselle said, "'Nice belt,'" and looked up quickly to get his first reaction.

Thomas smiled for her again.

She tilted her head. "Maybe a knock-knock joke. Knock, Knock."

"Who's there?"

"Little old lady."

"Little old lady who?" Thomas asked obediently.

Giselle was staring at Thomas. He knew looking away wasn't good. People looked away when they weren't telling the truth. He concentrated instead on the fringe of her eyelashes.

Reaching over, Giselle grabbed Thomas's knee. "I didn't know you could yodel." She tried to hold it in, but the laughter spilled out of her mouth. Shoulders shaking, Giselle said: "Come on, Thomas! *Little-o-lady-who*," she sang. "It's silly but silly-funny, don't you think?"

Thomas didn't know if the jokes were funny, because he wasn't thinking about them. He was thinking about what Giselle said earlier. As casually as someone would talk about the weather, the word "depressed" just rolled out of her mouth. They never said that word at Thomas's house. There were a thousand names for it: "sad," "tired," "low," "headache," "blue," "down," "moody," "sleepy," "exhausted," "not well." But *never* "depressed."

"Oh, Thomas." Giselle let her book drop and rested her hand, once again, on his knee. "It's worse than I thought."

But before Thomas could answer she pushed the book away on the counter and scrambled to her feet. "*Mon dieu!* Our hot chocolate!"

Chapter 6

The side door slammed and Aunt Sadie cursed as she struggled to step out of her boots.

"Why didn't you answer my calls?" she shouted. "Did you reach Helen?"

"I didn't answer because you didn't call me," Thomas's father shouted back, and then after a deep breath added in his regular voice, "Helen's still not answering her phone."

Aunt Sadie picked up Mr. Moran's cell phone from the kitchen table. She looked at the call history before pulling her phone out of her pocket.

"Mother of God," she said. "I've been calling heaven." She gave his father a look, one that dared him to say anything. "I meant Helen. Obviously."

Aunt Sadie took off her coat and put it on the counter. She pulled out Helen's chair and sat down before reaching over to grab Thomas's hand. She squeezed hard. It hurt and it felt good at the same time.

"Did you see her this morning?" Aunt Sadie asked Mr. Moran.

"For a short time before I left to teach."

"So she didn't sleep late," Aunt Sadie continued.

Sleeping late was what they said when Helen couldn't bring herself to get out of bed.

"Have you called the police?" Aunt Sadie asked.

His father glanced at Thomas before answering. It wasn't the kind of conversation he liked to have in front of his son. "She said she was going to try and run some errands, maybe she got held up. It's only been a few hours."

"A few hours? What's the definition of 'a few'?" Aunt Sadie said.

"More than a couple, but a small number."

"You said good-bye to her at, what . . ."

"I left at eight fifty."

"And it's past six. It's been more than eight hours since you've seen her, Brian. No one run errands for that long, especially Helen."

"She was up before I went to school," Thomas added, studying the surface of the table.

Aunt Sadie leaned toward Thomas. "Go on," she said.

Thomas considered. He was reluctant to mention his conversation with his mother because he wanted the dream to be for the two of them, the way it had been that morning. But things were different now.

His father was impatient. Thomas could tell by the way he snatched up Aunt Sadie's coat. Thomas waited for him to start for the landing, waited until his back was turned.

"She told me she'd had a dream that she was taking a trip."

"Thomas. Is that true?" His father was not hanging up Aunt Sadie's coat. He was not practicing first things first. "Why didn't you tell me earlier?"

"Because dreams are fanciful."

Thomas felt the caterpillars again. Inching their way along. For some reason, he thought about what he'd learned during another of their Ask Mrs. Evans lessons—that a caterpillar turned into liquid after it spun its chrysalis. A chrysalis was the hard shell in which a caterpillar lived until it transformed into a butterfly.

"Let's suppose for a moment that there's value in being fanciful," his father said, setting Aunt Sadie's coat back on the counter. "Tell us about your mother's dream."

"She was in an airport and when she looked at her ticket it didn't have a destination on it."

"The airport."

"Though it did have a seat assignment," Thomas added.

"Maybe we should go to the airport," his father said.

There was a knock at the front door, and Mr. Moran rushed to answer it, followed by Aunt Sadie and Thomas.

It was Mrs. Sharp, the old lady from across the street. Thomas liked her, though he couldn't say why. She had long gray hair that she kept piled on top of her head in a bun with some sort of stick in it, and she spoke with an accent.

"Mrs. Sharp. I'm sorry," Thomas's father was saying. "But this is not a good time. We're in the middle of . . . something."

"I saw Helen's car pull in," she said, walking through the hall to the kitchen. "I wanted to talk to you both."

Her eyes seemed to take in everything, like the little birds that hopped around the birdbath, turning their heads this way and that.

"She's not home," Mr. Moran said as they followed after her. "That's her sister's car."

"Oh dear, when I saw the car I assumed she was back . . ."

"This is Helen's sister, Sadie."

Mrs. Sharp turned so she could look at Thomas's aunt. "How like Helen you are. I'm Amalia. Amalia Sharp from across the street. You aren't . . . twins, are you? No, I can see now. Helen's the older."

"She's not, as it happens. I am."

"Of course. It's the *Weltschmerz*," Mrs. Sharp replied. "It ages you."

"*Weltschmerz?*"

"It's a German word. The literal translation is not satisfying. It means 'world pain,' but I think it is more about weariness than—"

"Mrs. Sharp, did you notice what time Helen left today?" Mr. Moran asked.

"I believe it was around noon." Thomas watched Mrs. Sharp, whose eyes were hopping from the table to his father to Aunt Sadie to the counter. She wasn't telling the truth, or maybe not the whole truth. Thomas could see things like that. Things that other people didn't see. Helen said it was because he was so quiet and thoughtful.

"It's just that she's . . . not back yet. We're concerned," Mr. Moran said.

"She rarely goes out, I know."

"Precisely. We're about to go look for her." Mr. Moran paused. "What was it you wanted to ask us?"

"Oh," Mrs. Sharp said. "Helen and I talked about my hiring Thomas and she suggested I come over so that we could all discuss it. I would need him for about fifteen minutes a day at dusk to help me feed the birds. Helen agreed that children are never too young to learn the value of work, and it's no—"

"I didn't know . . ." Mr. Moran looked confused. "You've been . . . talking with Helen?"

"You didn't know that we are friends, Helen and I? Your head is full of details, Mr. Moran. Missing one is not a crime." Mrs. Sharp looked at Thomas, lifting her eyebrows as if to say, "One or two."

"Do you want some coffee?" Thomas asked her.

"Thomas, this is hardly the time for pleasantries," Mr. Moran said.

But Thomas hadn't asked Mrs. Sharp if she wanted coffee to get her to stay. He asked her to see if she knew where the Morans kept their coffeepot. And as he suspected, those curious eyes turned directly to its home on the counter.

"We're wasting time," Mr. Moran said. "I'm going to the

airport, and...I'll discuss your offer with Helen when we find her."

Aunt Sadie put her hand on his father's arm to stop him. "We should call the police."

"Not until we've checked there first."

"I'm coming with you, then," his aunt said.

"Thomas, put on your coat," his father instructed.

"You can't be serious, Brian. We are not bringing Thomas." Aunt Sadie turned to Mrs. Sharp. "Would you...mind staying for an hour or so?"

"Sadie! I don't know that Mrs. Sharp has time—"

"It's *we* who don't have time, Brian." Aunt Sadie was taking charge. "As soon as we arrive, I'm contacting security," she said. Turning to face their neighbor, she repeated: "An hour or two...tops."

"We'll be fine, won't we, Thomas?" Mrs. Sharp said.

Mr. Moran handed Sadie her coat and retrieved his from the hook on the landing. "You have homework, Thomas. Make sure—"

"Brian! We have to get going."

Once the side door had closed behind them, Thomas and Mrs. Sharp sat down at the kitchen table. Thomas turned to face her so he could watch her eyes. "You were here with my mother today."

"What makes you say that?"

"You knew where the coffeepot was. You drank the coffee and cleaned the pot and her dishes."

"Yes, I did. I can't drink coffee as a rule—it's not good for my stomach, but once in a while..." Mrs. Sharp put her hand on Thomas's shoulder. "You pick up the crumbs your father misses, don't you?"

"Why didn't you tell him?"

"We meet when your father is busy at the college or has a meeting with an author away from home—and usually at my house. But today Helen wanted me to come here and help her identify birds. I didn't mention my visit because Helen... well, she asked me not to. I'm not sure why."

"Do you know where she is?"

"Of course I don't." She patted Thomas's cheek with her wrinkled hand. "I would never keep that from you or your father. You mustn't be concerned, Thomas. I'm quite sure she'll be home soon. Now..." She stood up and looked around. "Why don't you begin your homework and I'll see what I can put together for dinner."

Chapter 7
BEFORE

Thomas's baby sister, Sadie Rose, died two years ago when Thomas was eight. For weeks after, Helen lay in bed facing the wall. Thomas knew not to ask her or his father about the baby, so the questions stayed tucked inside him. At least until Tuesday or Thursday afternoons, when he saw her namesake, his aunt Sadie, who had started to help take care of him after the baby died.

It wasn't easy to question Aunt Sadie, who worked long hours and sometimes even Saturdays at the bank. On Tuesday and Thursday afternoons, however, she got off early and drove from the bank to the west side of town, where Thomas lived. Unless she had to stop by her apartment first; then she'd pick him up from school and take him to her place.

Aunt Sadie wore suits to the bank, but when she collected Thomas, she was almost always in what she called her tracksuit. Together, they ran errands, then went to the little gym in the shopping strip that was halfway between Aunt Sadie's apartment and the Morans' house.

Thomas usually sat beside the treadmill while Sadie did her workout. After that, he would follow her through the machines, carrying her towel and the index card of what weights she could handle in the overhead shoulder press and the leg curl.

To question his aunt about the baby—to ask her any question really—Thomas had to be very careful with his timing. If Aunt Sadie was on the treadmill, for example, and he waited too long, she was too out of breath to talk—and questions irritated her. But if he asked too soon, she couldn't concentrate because she was still thinking about her boss, Mr. Montgomery.

"Who has the degree in accounting? With distinction?" she'd ask Thomas. And then answer the question herself. "You do, Sadie. His economics degree is not nearly as applicable to banking." Or, "Why am I not in charge of the year-to-date reports? Because he micro-manages everything, that's why."

Thomas did not know what micro-managing was, but he did know that Aunt Sadie needed to ask herself these questions before he got to ask any of his.

It was Tuesday, two days after Giselle dug the hole and told Thomas about what happens to your bloodstream when you pet a dog or nurse a baby, and the day after Helen sat on the floor with Frenchy. There was something Thomas very much wanted to ask Aunt Sadie.

When she hit the incline button on the treadmill, he crossed his fingers for luck behind his back. "Tell me again what was wrong with the baby?"

"I assume you mean Helen's baby... your sister." Aunt Sadie's face was red but she was not huffing yet.

Thomas nodded.

"When she was born, they did some tests. They give all babies the same tests. They found out she had a heart defect. We've talked about this, Thomas. She had CCHD—critical congenital heart disease."

There was a difference between talking about something and understanding it.

"But how did she get it?"

"We don't know. It's very rare."

His courage failed him. What Thomas really wanted to ask was if Baby Sadie had lived and his mother had breastfed her, would she have been all right? Was this oxytocin that Giselle mentioned like medicine? Did it make the clouds go away?

Chapter 8

The day Helen disappeared, Aunt Sadie slept over, which she never did. The next morning Thomas came downstairs and found her and his father in the kitchen.

Mr. Moran repeated what he'd told Thomas when they'd come home from the airport: "Your mother has gone somewhere, and we don't know where. We searched for her, but we didn't find her."

Aunt Sadie lifted her head from her crossed arms on the table. "We contacted airport security; we called the police, too. Everyone is looking for her, Thomas. A detective is coming over this morning."

"Will he need a picture of her? Like on TV?"

"Yes, but we'll take care of that," his father said. "You'll be at school."

"School?"

"There's no point in your staying home, Thomas. You'll be better off at school—"

"That is fanciful!" Thomas used his fist to pound an exclamation point onto the kitchen table. "You do not know where I'll be better off!"

For a moment, everyone was still. It was not like Thomas to make a fuss.

"You're right." Stroking Thomas's arm, Aunt Sadie said, "We don't know anything, really. But we'll be in and out. We don't want to leave you alone."

"She flew somewhere. I told you! You should check all the flights."

"We are, Duck. We are," Aunt Sadie said, using her favorite pet name for her nephew.

"I'll stay with Mrs. Sharp. She's said she's happy to watch me anytime."

"I know. But we may need to call on her tonight. Please, Thomas?" His father was begging, which he never did.

"As soon as we talk to the detective, we're going back to the airport," Aunt Sadie said in her bank voice. "Don't worry. We'll find her."

Thomas waited for his father to tell Aunt Sadie not to presume. What evidence did they have that they would find his mother? But his father said nothing.

Thomas went to get his coat.

"I'll drive you to school." Aunt Sadie put on Helen's big

down coat and started her car from inside the house, the way she liked to do in winter.

Pressing her hand into his back, Thomas's aunt hustled him into the passenger seat of the now-warm car.

He watched from the window as Giselle left her house and ran to her mother's car. She had on a skirt with blue tights underneath and her purple puffy jacket. Pulling her hair out of her collar as she ran, she stopped short in the driveway when she saw them: "Thomas!" she shouted. "Bonne journée! Have a great day!"

Ms. Dover rolled down her car window. "Hello, Thomas. And..." She lowered her sunglasses. "Is that...Helen?"

"I'm Sadie. Thomas's aunt. We met last Halloween. I'm sorry, but we're...late."

"Of course. I remember you, Sadie. We won't keep you. Giselle's last-minute costume changes—" She broke off and gave them a big wave that seemed to encompass the neighborhood. "Isn't this sunshine lovely?"

Thomas and Aunt Sadie could hear the Dovers laughing as Giselle's mother rolled up her window.

After they drove away, Aunt Sadie got into the driver's seat and leaned her head against the steering wheel. "Just so you know, Thomas," she said finally. "That is normal."

They drove to school, and though Aunt Sadie dropped him off at the entrance, she didn't leave. Thomas watched her car circle the parking lot before coming to a stop in one of the visitor spaces. Then he spotted Martin waiting for him on the front steps, students streaming past.

"Here's something for you to count," Thomas said, tugging on Martin's shirt.

"What?"

"The number of seconds from the time we get in the classroom until Mrs. Evans leaves."

Counting time was Martin's favorite. You could surprise him with the question "How long have you been alive?" and by the time he answered "Let's see, that would be..." he could give you the time down to the second. "3,834 days, 11 hours, 42 minutes...and, as of right now"—he'd glance at his luminous digital watch face that kept exact time—"37 seconds."

"Okay."

When they got to the classroom, Martin consulted his watch and the boys took their seats just as the bell rang.

Mrs. Evans was writing a journal question on her whiteboard. "That's enough, George," she said without turning around.

"What? I'm just sitting here." George stuffed a giant rubber tarantula into his desk.

She put down her marker and turned to face the class. "Why is it that when Bella screams, I immediately think of George Panagopoulos?"

"I don't know," George mumbled. "Are you sexist?"

Mrs. Evans was not a fan of mumbling, but her reply was interrupted by a knock on the door and Principal Bowen leaning in. "Mrs. Evans, can you go down to the office for a conference?" She glanced at Thomas. "I'll stay with the class."

Martin whispered, "Three hundred and twenty-seven seconds."

"Mary Mallender. Will you bring me up to speed?"

"Yes, Principal Bowen. Mrs. Evans was asking why every time Bella screams, it has to do with George."

"And I was suggesting that I am the victim of profiling," George remarked, this time quite clearly.

"No, you didn't," Mary corrected him. "You said she was sexist."

What George had really done was *ask* if Mrs. Evans was sexist. Mary Mallender was a know-it-all, but she didn't *really* know it all. To be more precise, her slight mistake changed the meaning entirely.

Principal Bowen didn't care about who was being profiled or who was sexist. She led them through the Pledge of Allegiance and sat at Mrs. Evans's desk while the announcements were read over the intercom. Following that, she gazed at the class over her bifocals and said, "I see a journal prompt on the board. The next thing I'd like to see is you busy answering it."

Thomas got out his journal and wrote the date at the top of the page. Yesterday at this time, his mother had not left the house. Mrs. Sharp had said she left around noon. Yesterday at this time, she was still safe. Now, only God knew. Well. What Aunt Sadie had said, after his father had tucked Thomas back into bed last night and he'd gotten out and lay down by the cold air register so he could hear them talking, was, "Only God knows where Helen's gone."

Thomas looked at the page in his journal. He didn't need to write about what happened yesterday as they were instructed to do. Aunt Sadie would be telling Mrs. Evans right now.

He felt a wriggling deep inside and put his hand over his stomach to quiet it. He knew from his book about butterflies that he and Mrs. Sharp had looked at last night that caterpillars wriggled as they spun their chrysalises. She had pointed out that what seemed like one tiny point where each chrysalis attached itself to a branch was, in reality, dozens of tiny hooks. The hooks were firmly embedded or the chrysalis would fall and break when the wind blew hard, for example.

He thought the caterpillars must be attaching themselves to the top of his stomach, where they would hang upside down like a row of Houdinis, soon to be wrapped in a layer of gauze.

Chapter 9
BEFORE

Just before Thanksgiving, Helen's doctor had decided to try another new medicine because she still wasn't feeling better. Thomas's father had explained to him that it was always hard for Helen when they switched her medication—her body needed time to adjust while they waited for the new medicine to take effect.

It had only been a few days, but as Thomas studied his mother as they ate dinner, he couldn't help but wish that the medicine would hurry up. The clouds were still in her eyes.

When they were finished, Helen said, "Brian, you go back downstairs to work. We'll clean up."

"You sure?"

"I can still wash dishes."

Helen pushed herself up from the kitchen table and went over to the sink. The water gurgled. Mr. Moran squeezed

Thomas's arm as Thomas stood and placed the silverware on his plate. When he looked up, his father was gone.

Thomas hurried back and forth, and soon the plates were rinsed and put into the dishwasher. Helen began filling the sink for the pots, pans, and glasses they washed by hand. When the bubbles threatened to spill over, Thomas reached around his mother and turned off the tap.

"Should I wash?" he asked.

Helen shook her head, leaning so far over the sink that the tips of her hair brushed the top of the foamy water. She didn't want Thomas to see the tears that slid from the corners of her eyes down her face. They didn't seem like real tears to Thomas, but more like a leak, like water seeping out of a crack. "Rivulet." That was the word.

Pressing the backs of her hands to her eye sockets, Helen said: "Hand the dishes to me. I'll wash and you can dry."

Thomas handed a casserole dish to his mother, who took it in her hands and dipped it into the soapy water. Even though the water was steaming, she held the dish below the surface.

Thomas didn't know what she was waiting for. He busied himself as long as he could, returning the salt and pepper shakers to their tray on the counter, sweeping the crumbs around the breadbasket into his hand, setting the butter dish in the refrigerator door.

"Are you okay?" Thomas could see a trail on the side of her face, but the rivulet had stopped. Helen just nodded and swiped at the casserole dish with her sponge before rinsing it off and handing it to Thomas. Dripping.

Grabbing the towel from the handle of the fridge, Thomas dried it. By the time he had placed it on the counter, Helen was holding out his father's water glass. More water dripped onto the floor. Thomas chose to ignore it. He'd wipe it up after they'd finished.

Just as his fingers touched the glass, Helen let go and it slipped out of his grasp to the floor and broke.

"Thomas!" Helen scolded.

He knelt to the ground to pick up the pieces.

"Get back! You're in your stocking feet. Sit on the kitchen chair."

Helen moved as if she would put Thomas on the chair herself, but her slippered foot found the puddle and she too fell to the floor—taking the same path as the glass had—before he could move to help her.

Thomas saw that blood ran down her arm. It was more than a rivulet. She stayed sitting where she was and gazed at it the way she did at a ladybug crawling on her finger.

Thomas ran to get his father.

Mr. Moran didn't ask questions. He led the way back up the stairs, yanking the whole roll off the paper towel dispenser when he reached the kitchen. "You need to hold your arm high," he said, crouching down next to Helen. "Oh my God, this is deep. Thomas, go get the first aid kit."

Thomas ran upstairs, but the white plastic box was not under the sink in his parents' bathroom.

"Can't find it!" he screamed from the top of the stairs.

"Come back here, Thomas. Deep breaths...Okay, listen closely. I need you to run next door and ask Ms. Dover if she has gauze, and—" Thomas's father couldn't crouch any longer. He stood, still holding up Helen's arm. "Try to help me, Helen. You have to keep your arm above your heart. Butterfly bandages, Thomas. See if she has any. Go!"

"It's not his fault," Helen said as Thomas struggled with the deadbolt. "The glass slipped out of my hand."

Thomas freed the lock, flung open the door, and ran. Down the driveway and onto the sidewalk. Through the curtain of bushes that separated the Dovers' house from the street. Throwing himself at their door, he smacked it with the flat of his hand and then rang the doorbell, pressing down as hard as he could.

With his ear to the door he heard music. Loud pulsing music.

"Keep your *pantalons* on!" Giselle threw open the door, her face flushed, wearing strings of flower leis around her neck. "Thomas!" she cried, pulling him in and tossing a string of flowers around his neck as well. "Come join our dance party." Frenchy stood on his hind legs pawing the air as if he, too, wanted Thomas to dance.

Pulling his hand away, Thomas shook free and ran toward the source of the music. In the middle of the living room, Giselle's mother was jumping on a mini-trampoline. "You have to give this a go, Thomas," she shouted. "It's very stimulating to the adrenals."

Thomas searched for the stereo. He found the remote and hit the red power button.

Giselle's mother bounced off the trampoline. "Thomas, sweet, what is it?"

"My mother's cut herself, Ms. Dover! My father needs some gauze and a butterfly bandage. She was handing me a glass to dry, but it slipped."

Crossing the room, Ms. Dover paused at the bottom of the stairs. "I'll get my first aid kit. You should call me Nadine, Thomas. I'd prefer it."

As Ms. Dover ran upstairs, Giselle lifted the lei from Thomas's neck and dropped it and her own to the floor. She put her arms around Thomas. "You're shivering," she said quietly.

Breaking away to get her jacket, Giselle threw it over Thomas's shoulders and put her arm around him as they walked back to the Morans' house.

Ms. Dover rushed past them on the sidewalk. When Thomas and Giselle arrived, she was squatting next to Helen at the kitchen table, pressing gauze to her hand and wrapping it with more. Mr. Moran made a slow circle around them with the broom, looking for stray pieces of glass.

"Now it looks like you've got a paw," Ms. Dover said, lifting Helen's chin with her finger. "Helen? Are you okay?" As soon as she removed her finger, Helen's chin dropped back down. Thomas noticed the tears leaking again.

Ms. Dover stood. "Brian, this will need stitches. It will reopen, especially on her palm. I—"

"Thomas," his father instructed. "Why don't you take Giselle upstairs and show her your sketchbook?"

"I know a good urgent care facility," Ms. Dover continued. "I think it's still open."

Thomas led the way upstairs. He pulled out the chair to his desk and opened his sketchbook. Giselle sat down. Thomas had never seen her so quiet. He left her in his room to take his place by the cold air register.

"Helen, what have they got you on?" When his mother didn't answer, Ms. Dover repeated her question to his father.

"None of the new drugs have worked. Helen's depression has been so treatment resistant that Dr. Beecher is trying one of the old tricyclics. As you know, it always takes a while to—"

"But was she clear of her other meds? What about her diet? You have to be careful with interactions. Even citrus can—"

"Helen is getting very good care, Nadine."

"I'm so sorry."

"Thanks for your help. We're fine now."

"You know, Brian. There's a difference between people pitying you and people feeling compassion for your struggle. You don't have to shut everyone out. Thomas—"

"I wouldn't have sent Thomas over, but he couldn't find our first aid kit. It's just a cut."

"Why don't you let me stay here while you take Helen?"

"That's not necessary. I'll call Helen's sister. Really, Nadine. We're fine. I'm sorry we interrupted your evening."

Thomas returned to his bedroom, where Giselle was still paging through his sketchbook.

"Why only butterflies?" she asked.

Thomas shrugged. He didn't know why.

"Giselle," Ms. Dover called up the stairs. "We need to go now."

Giselle took hold of Thomas's shoulders. "This is how the French do it." She pulled Thomas close. "Both good-bye and hello are the same. You lean in..." Giselle pressed her cheek to his. "Always offer your right cheek," she continued. "And you don't actually kiss, you kiss the air." Thomas heard the sound of Giselle's lips smacking next to his ear.

"Now the other side." More smacking. "Tonight, I say, 'À bientôt, mon ami,' which means 'See you soon, my friend.' Have you got it?"

Thomas nodded.

"Thomas?" Giselle leaned in, pressing her forehead to Thomas's, pressing her nose to his nose. "Will you draw one for me? A butterfly."

"Okay."

"A butterfly that looks like...what I would look like if I were a butterfly?"

"Okay."

After Aunt Sadie had tucked him in, Thomas lay in the dark thinking about the Dovers and how Giselle had been dancing on a weekday night to loud music with flowers around her neck while her mother bounced on a trampoline in their living room.

When he saw Aunt Sadie again, he would ask her—was that normal, too?

Chapter 10

When the doorbell rang that first afternoon after Helen went away, Thomas didn't even have time to get up from his chair in the kitchen where he was working on his homework to answer it. His father rushed by so fast, he almost knocked into Thomas.

"Stay here," his father said, closing the kitchen door behind him.

The way he rushed made the butterfly chrysalises rattle in Thomas's stomach. They felt heavy and solid and Thomas did not want to make any sudden movements, so he stood up slowly and opened the door just a crack to listen.

"Mr. Moran? I'm Officer Celia Grant from the Ottawa County Police Department. Detective Freeman sent me. We found your car, sir. It was at the airport."

"I knew it! Thank God. Now all we have to do is figure out what flight she took."

"May I come in?"

His father stepped aside, and once Officer Grant was in the foyer, she said, "It's not the city airport, but a private airport out by the river."

"I don't understand."

"Hawks' Run caters to small private planes. It has one airstrip."

"So . . . you're saying Helen took a private plane?"

"No. I . . . I'm sorry, but we still don't know what your wife did. We got a call from the security officer at the airport about a car abandoned in the parking lot."

It was a good thing that Officer Grant did not presume. Maybe they trained that out of you at the school for police officers. Thomas had heard that on police shows: "Just the facts, ma'am."

"He could see that a purse and cell phone were still in the locked car and the license plate didn't match anyone's who works at or uses the airport. So he called us."

"Where did you say this airport was? I've never heard of it. Did you say that Helen left her purse in the car? She's quite forgetful as a rule. I'll get my coat."

"I am sorry, sir, but we're organizing a search of the area and no one is allowed access at the moment. I do need to go over a few details with you."

"What do you mean 'no one is allowed'? She's my wife. We're talking about our car."

"I'm sure you understand the delicacy of the matter. We

can't allow people to walk over the ground and potentially disrupt the search. What will be helpful is if you'd go over what happened yesterday. I know you spoke to Detective Freeman this morning, but in light of this new—"

"I already explained what happened." Mr. Moran spoke slowly, as if he were talking to Thomas, who'd just told him something fantastical.

"Would you mind going over it again? I need to take notes about what everyone was doing."

"What possible bearing can that have on—"

"Because your wife is now a missing person. Officially. And while it is just a formality, we need to rule out that any family members were involved. Is your wife's sister here?"

"No. She left to get a change of clothes at her apartment. Do you want me to call her?"

"That's not necessary, but it would be good if she could stop by the station. I'll be there until eight tonight."

Thomas listened as his father recounted yesterday's events one more time before he stepped out from behind the kitchen door and said, "You need something that smells like her, don't you? For the dogs."

"Thomas. I'll handle this."

"Is this . . . this is Thomas?"

Thomas walked slowly toward the officer, careful not to disturb the chrysalises.

"Thomas, I told you to stay in the kitchen."

"With your permission, Mr. Moran, I need to ask Thomas

a question. It might have some bearing on your wife's whereabouts."

"I'd rather you asked me. Thomas is...He gets very anx—"

"How about if I ask you both?"

Mr. Moran turned to look at Thomas. Without saying anything, he was asking Thomas if that was okay, if *he* would be okay. Thomas nodded. He couldn't look the officer in the eye, but settled instead on a bright twist of fabric poking out of her jacket pocket. She must have followed his gaze, because she pulled it out and offered it to him, cradling it in the palm of her hand.

"My daughter gave me this," she said as Thomas picked it up to examine it more closely. "Lily's too young to understand it's not the sort of thing a police officer can wear."

It was, in fact, a butterfly. A tiny blue butterfly whose wings were clipped into the metal prongs of a bobby pin. The sort of pin that Helen used to put up her hair.

"It reminds me of a Karner blue, Thomas. Do you know that one?"

Thomas nodded. He knew it very well. "They are endangered," he said, handing the butterfly back to Officer Grant.

Putting his arm around his son, Mr. Moran pulled Thomas toward him. There was no point in telling his father about the chrysalises; but since Thomas was their sole protector, he had to pull away and stand up straight.

Officer Grant reached into her jacket pocket again and she

pulled out a plastic bag. It was the kind Thomas's family put their leftover bread in.

"This was on the front seat as well." She held up the bag. Inside was the Revolutionnaire DVD that Helen and Thomas liked to watch. Before. Written on an orange piece of notepaper torn from the pad on their refrigerator were the words "For Thomas."

"Thomas?" His father took the bag. "Do you know what this means? It appears to be your mother's cooking DVD, the one that goes with that food processor."

"We watched it together. You can learn a lot about cooking even if you don't own . . ." Thomas trailed off.

Mr. Moran returned the DVD to Officer Grant and said, "Thomas, please go back to the kitchen."

Thomas did as he was told, scraping the chair as he sat down. Then he picked up his pencil and bent his head, pretending to study.

"This is a lot to take in," his father said.

"I know. I'm very sorry. Given what we know about this location . . . The airport is near a bridge that spans the river. It's a train trestle really." Officer Grant continued talking in a low voice. "I'm very sorry to tell you this. Others have used the bridge—well . . . they've jumped off the bridge."

There was a silence. Then Thomas heard his father say, "How many others?"

"Three over the past couple of years."

"Which might lead you to the conclusion—easily a false one—that my wife, given her medical issues . . ."

"We believe it's a possibility, Mr. Moran. But at this point it's just one possibility. Detective Freeman wouldn't organize a land search and call in the mobile tracking unit if we were certain."

"Of course not. Forgive me. It's...she's my wife. I want to search, too."

"The best thing at the moment is to let the dogs do their work and not be distracted by new scents. Speaking of scents, Thomas is right. It would be helpful if we had something for the dogs to work with. It's very difficult for them to pick up scents in the cold. Did your wife have a particular perfume she liked to wear?"

Mr. Moran shook his head.

"Maybe what she wore to sleep, then?"

"Do women wear perfume to sleep?"

"No...I meant pajamas."

"Oh, of course. I'll get them."

"Thank you."

"So, at this point, you have no solid evidence. I mean, someone could have stolen her car and..."

Thomas froze. Was his father allowing for something he didn't know to be true?

"At the moment, we don't think there was foul play involved. Nothing was broken. There was no sign of a struggle. I'm...so sorry. For both you and your son, this is frightening and upsetting...I...I've found..." There was a pause in the conversation. "There's a number on this card," Officer

Grant resumed. "It's for a support group for families of people with...who suffer from...It might help to know there are others—"

"Thank you, Officer Grant." There was a silence. Then his father: "I'll go get a pair of her pajamas."

Thomas was in his chair at the kitchen table, holding his pencil, when his father came in. He sat across from Thomas where he always sat, looking at a small white card. Then he set it facedown, pulled out his phone, and punched two buttons. Speed dial. Thomas knew he was calling Aunt Sadie.

"Why doesn't she pick up?" Mr. Moran asked the cupboard over Thomas's head. Turning his phone to the side, he tapped out a text message.

May Day? S.O.S?

Thomas felt the slightest shift in his stomach. The chrysalises! Then an increase in pressure at the bottom of one, a crack traveling upward.

It was far too early. He and Mrs. Sharp had read that it took up to a month for a caterpillar to become a butterfly once it had spun its chrysalis. While that might be true, Thomas knew what he was feeling.

He stood up, holding the back of his chair. Maybe if he lay down it would help.

"Thomas? Are you okay? Take a deep breath to calm yourself. Please. We'll get through this."

"I'm...going to lie down," he said. And he would have

gone to his room, but just as he reached the bottom of the stairs, the doorbell rang again.

Thomas held on to the round ball that was the beginning of the stair rail. Frozen. Forcing himself to breathe.

Mr. Moran strode down the hallway and flung the door open.

Giselle burst in and said, "Thomas! I'm so glad you're home."

His father stood with his hand on the door, staring at Giselle.

"Thomas?" she said, peering in at him. "Are you all right?"

Thomas felt behind him for a stair to sit on.

"Thomas can't play right now, Gretchen." His father was angry. He was being interrupted when what he needed to do was find Aunt Sadie right away.

"I'm Giselle, not Gretchen. And I haven't come to play. I have something for Thomas."

"Oh. Well. Thank you for that." Mr. Moran took the package that Giselle produced from underneath her arm. "Good-bye."

"Don't you want to know what it is, Thomas?"

"No, as a matter of fact. He doesn't."

Thomas noted this second journey of his father's into speculation. It turned out to be true that Thomas had other things on his mind, but his father had no way of knowing that.

Mr. Moran pressed the package into Thomas's arms. It

was big and blocky, wrapped in brown paper, and tied with a string. "Take this upstairs with you, Thomas."

Thomas held the package across his chest like a shield. Holding his back straight, he stood up and took a step backward. Up the steps. Very slowly. Holding on to each spindle in the stair rail.

"As you can see . . . Thomas isn't feeling well. He needs to lie down."

Giselle studied Thomas; though he knew he should not look away, he couldn't hold her gaze.

"But—" Even she was no match for Thomas's father, who was herding her back to the open door.

The door closed and his father said, "You'll be okay?"

Thomas nodded, counting his breath, taking his time stepping backward up the stairs as his father returned to the kitchen and his cell phone. When Thomas reached his bedroom, he eased himself onto his bed, making sure to lie straight so he didn't disturb the chrysalises.

These butterflies have terrible timing.

Chapter 11
BEFORE

Thomas was seven the year Helen found the DVD of the Swiss chef Philippe Duprée for twenty-five cents at the Super Thrift. Narrated by Philippe, it explained how to cook using the eleven-cup-capacity classic Revolutionnaire food processor. Helen said it didn't matter that they didn't own a food processor. You could still learn a great deal from Philippe.

Thomas often wondered what it was about the chef that made him and his mother feel so warm and calm. Maybe it was Philippe's accent, or that he always knew what to do next and never got frustrated, even when he made a mistake. Philippe's gray hair was parted in the middle and went down to his shoulders. His beard was gray as well; the only time Thomas had ever seen anyone with hair like that was in the picture-book Bible handed down from Grandma Torini. Everyone had hair like that in the picture-book Bible.

When Thomas came home from school, he'd have a snack

and then Helen would put on Philippe's DVD, in which he demonstrated the wonders of the Revolutionnaire.

"What should we make today?" his mother would ask as they cuddled up together on the bed she shared with Thomas's father. "Pizza crust?"

"Pizza crust is so easy," Thomas murmured. "Even the first time Philippe made it, it worked perfectly."

Philippe liked to tell a story about every single recipe. "I never made pizza crust before I came to the United States. One day I saw zis very famous rock star enter my restaurant in Las Vegas and ask for pizza. I told her I didn't know how. She walked away, so upset that I called after her, 'No, let me try!' and I made it in zis." Philippe pointed to the Revolutionnaire with wonder. "And now you can make it, too. Even if I can't be in the kitchen with you, you will still get an excellent result."

"Cinnamon rolls," Thomas decided. Helen pressed a button on the remote and then forwarded the DVD until there was Philippe in his TV kitchen, a long white apron tied at the waist in a bunny knot. Philippe always wore an apron, though Thomas never saw him spill.

"Zees sweet rolls are so easy," Philippe told them for the hundredth time. "Zey take me back to my childhood in Lausanne and a delicious memory of my parents' pastry shop."

Philippe picked up the work bowl of the food processor and locked it into place. Then he picked up a short sharp blade—very carefully—and said: "Zis is ze dough blade."

After he'd secured the blade, he poured in the flour, salt, and sugar, placed the lid on top and also locked it into place.

Looking down at the processor, Philippe spoke almost to himself: "Here we go." Thomas and Helen watched Philippe pulse together the flour, salt, and sugar before pouring the yeast mixture into the feed tube attached to the lid and holding his finger down on the pulse button for fifteen seconds.

After he was done, he pushed the Revolutionnaire to the side and produced a bowl filled with fluffy dough he'd made earlier so his viewers didn't have to wait for it to rise.

As Philippe dumped the sticky dough onto the pastry board, he said "Here we go" again, and so did Thomas and his mother. Things were about to get messy.

Thomas's father wasn't a fan of the messiness of baking. There were cracks and crevices that flour could reach that fingers and sponges and even vacuums could not. He would have liked watching the DVD, where everything remained clean and shiny.

"Now, before we shape zees, we add some more butter to ze dough. Of course, we also want to butter our pan here...A little extra butter never hurt ze cinnamon rolls."

This was how they learned the language of Philippe. If Aunt Sadie was dressing the salad and Helen thought she should add more, she would say: "A little extra butter never hurt the cinnamon rolls, Sadie." Or when Thomas learned to tie a bunny knot, he looked up at his father and said: "Just follow my instructions and you will get an excellent result."

Once, Helen made the cinnamon rolls by hand with Thomas as her assistant and served them to Aunt Sadie and Mr. Moran after church.

"You should start a bakery, Helen...seriously." Aunt Sadie kept talking, even though her mouth was full. "I would pay for this."

"Only if I were available to keep the kitchen up to code," Mr. Moran said.

"Why does the kitchen need a code?" Thomas asked.

His father ruffled his hair and held out his plate for another roll. "I was teasing your mother, Thomas. A bakery kitchen needs to be very clean so the customers don't get sick. 'Up to code' means it has passed inspection."

"I'm not that bad, Brian."

"No, Sadie's right." Mr. Moran set his plate down and smiled. "You are that good."

Chapter 12

Thomas lay on his bed, absorbed in what was happening inside him. It had been almost dark when Giselle brought the package. Now the streetlight shone in the window. He wasn't good at counting minutes the way Martin was. He had heard his father's voice on the phone, the front door open and close, and voices in the hall. Then silence.

"It is dark already," he said aloud as he ran his fingers over his belly. The cracks were traveling. They didn't hurt. The shells were like a fingernail. It didn't hurt when you trimmed your nails; just as it hadn't hurt when the cracking began.

Thomas lay very still, paying close attention, until he heard a knock on his door.

It was Mrs. Sharp. "Thomas, are you awake? I've brought you a cup of chamomile tea."

Thomas sat up and took the teacup. He sipped to be polite but was surprised to find that he liked the sweet taste.

"Your father is meeting your aunt at the police station. Would you like me to fix you some dinner?" she asked.

"I'm not hungry," Thomas whispered, sipping a bit more. Butterflies liked sugar water.

Mrs. Sharp pulled out his desk chair and set it near the bed, pressing her knees into his comforter as she sat.

"Why are you holding your stomach? Are you in pain?"

Thomas shook his head. "My mother has disappeared," he told Mrs. Sharp, setting down the teacup and taking sips of breath instead.

"I know." Mrs. Sharp took Thomas's hand and squeezed it. "We are all very concerned."

"I should be out looking for her," he said. He closed his eyes and lay back down.

"I know you want to, dear, but it's best to let the police handle it. They are very good at their jobs." Thomas felt Mrs. Sharp's hands tucking the covers around him. "What's this package?"

"It's from Giselle. She brought it over. Just before...I had to lie down."

"Would you like me to open it?"

Thomas nodded. He listened to Mrs. Sharp untying string, to the crinkle of brown paper. The paper fell to the floor.

Then there was no sound. Mrs. Sharp was waiting for him.

Thomas opened his eyes and as he struggled to sit up, she reached behind him to arrange his pillows so he could lean against them. Then she handed him a big spiral-bound note-book with drawings all over the front: houses, animals, birds, flowers. There was a lemony yellow sun in the sky as big as a tennis ball. Giselle had used fancy stencils to make the title, just like the ones they had in art class: "*The Big Book of Laughter and Happy Things.*"

"Do you want to see what's inside?"

Thomas nodded. He had no idea what Giselle would put inside.

Flipping through the pages, Mrs. Sharp said: "It appears to be blank. It must be for you to fill with drawings."

Thomas yawned, wondering if the sudden rush of air would affect his butterflies.

"Can butterflies migrate even if it's cold outside?"

"I've no doubt they find their way."

After Mrs. Sharp left, and his father and Aunt Sadie came in to kiss him good-night, Thomas crept out of bed and opened his window a crack. Just in case.

The next morning the heaviness in his stomach was gone and he felt sure that the butterflies had been born and found their way, like Mrs. Sharp said.

All but one. One butterfly had wanted to stay. Thomas could feel something dry and papery, like wings unfolding. Though it wasn't an obvious choice, he named his butterfly Dave.

Chapter 13
BEFORE

When Thomas started kindergarten, Helen began working part-time at a day-care center. The kindergarten program was only a half day, so Thomas went to day care with Helen in the morning and the bus picked him up to go to school after lunchtime. Helen was home by the time the school bus dropped him off in the afternoon. It was at the day-care center that Thomas met Dave. Even though Dave was only three, Thomas saw their similarities. For one, Dave's favorite place to stand was next to his mother, wrapping her full skirt around him like a bat enfolding itself in its wings. During sharing time, Dave sat on her lap.

Dave sucked on the three inside fingers of his right hand. Thomas had sucked the cuff of his sleeve: when that was forbidden, he had learned to wait until nighttime and suck on his bedsheet instead. No one seemed to care much that Dave put his fingers in his mouth. That is, until cold and flu season hit;

then it was Thomas's job to help him remember not to do it. It was no easy task to convince a three-year-old to deny himself his greatest source of comfort, conveniently located at the end of his arm.

Thomas was there for the morning transfer at seven when Dave's hands were pried from the lapels of his mother's blazer only to attach themselves to one of Helen's chunky necklaces.

"Dave." Thomas attempted to distract him. "Do you want to play with the trains?"

Dave shook his head. But even Dave wasn't allowed to remain with Helen all morning. When she put him down, he would disappear, and it was also Thomas's job to keep track of him. Fortunately, Dave's movements were predictable. Thomas usually found him in the story corner, tucked behind the milk crates filled with picture books. He knew Thomas would follow and read him a story. Though he was five, Thomas read at the third-grade level.

"Do you want to read about your favorite steam engine?" Thomas flipped over an empty crate and sat down on it. "You're not supposed to suck on your fingers, remember?"

Dave said, "You're not the boss of me." It was impressive how Dave could make himself understood around his fingers.

Thomas couldn't imagine himself being the boss of anyone. He pointed to Dave's other hand. "What are you holding?"

Dave relaxed his fingers, revealing a round, gray stone.

"I see. A dinosaur egg."

Dave shook his head. "Too small."

"No it's not. There were small dinosaurs, too, you know."

Dave seemed to take this idea into consideration. The sucking noises grew louder. "No," he said finally. "There were not."

"Yes." Thomas spoke in what he hoped sounded like a grown-up voice. "There were. I'll show you if you don't believe me."

They found a book about dinosaurs on the table. He set it on Dave's lap and watched him take his fingers out of his mouth to turn the pages. He tried to not think about how annoyed his mother's boss, Mrs. Purdy, would be if she knew Dave was getting saliva all over the pages.

"There." Thomas pointed at what looked like a cross between a dinosaur and a bird. "This one is small. It's a microraptor. Only as long as your arm."

"Why does it have wings on its legs?" Dave wanted to know, and before Thomas could stop him, he inserted his fingers back in his mouth.

"Microraptors had four wings," Thomas explained, reading the caption. "Two on its body and two on its legs, but they couldn't really fly. They just glided from tree to tree."

"Some squirrels can glide like that," Dave told him.

"That's true." As Thomas considered ways to get Dave to turn the pages again, Helen came up behind them.

"David Alexander Stanley Cup Playoffs," Helen said.

She always came up with invented names for the students—they loved it.

"That is not my name!" Dave responded, giggling with delight.

"Well, then, David Alexander Balthazar Rumpelstiltskin, please take that finger-flavored lollipop out of your mouth." Bending over, Helen kissed Dave on the top of the head and whispered something in his ear as she gently removed the fingers from his mouth.

Helen was the only person Dave would allow to do this. He'd been known to bite his own fingers to deny them exit.

Helen was the boss of him.

"I tried," Thomas told her later when they were eating their lunch together in the break room. "It's hard."

"I know, sweet. He has to be very distracted to stop. If he's not distracted, he's thinking about—you know—his troubles."

"What troubles?"

"Not real troubles, just... things that make him anxious. Like worrying that his mom is not coming back. Sucking his fingers calms him down." Helen ran a carrot around her container of hummus and offered it to Thomas. "Believe me, there are plenty of adults who would do it if they could."

"Adults still want to suck their fingers?"

"Well, not exactly. But we do get anxious. For instance, I don't love speaking in front of a group. Like at Parents' Night. It makes me feel like there are butterflies in my stomach."

"What do you do instead of sucking on your fingers?" Thomas asked, biting into his carrot.

"Me? Well, I try to think of something else. Something nice."

"Like what?"

"Like... butterflies. In fact, before your bus gets here, why don't you draw one for me?"

"I don't know how."

"We have a book that shows you. Draw one of those little blue ones they're trying to save up north. The Karner blue."

"Is it in the book?" Thomas asked, crinkling the tin foil from their sandwiches into a ball and putting it back inside their paper lunch bag.

"I doubt it. But it's the same shape as the other butterflies. Just... smaller. I know..." Helen disappeared into Mrs. Purdy's office. She came back out with three blue colored pencils. "This is from the teacher's set," she told Thomas, handing them to him. "It's a tiny thing, not much bigger than a quarter. And it's all blue. Different shades of blue."

They stood in the doorway to the break room, looking out at the children sitting at low tables eating their lunches.

"Can you show me one on your phone?" Thomas asked, hoping to keep his mother by his side a little longer. But Helen was already distracted by a crying child.

"Later," she said. "For now, use your imagination."

Chapter 14

Thomas's father and aunt didn't go to work the week Helen disappeared. Aunt Sadie slept over in the spare bedroom and every morning Thomas found her teacups and his father's coffee mugs clustered on the kitchen table like captured checkers.

Officer Grant stopped by on Saturday—no butterfly pin, Thomas checked—and told his father and Aunt Sadie that they'd eliminated all family members from their inquiries. She apologized again, and his father said he was the one who should apologize; he realized she was only doing her job.

Officer Grant told them that the police had finished with their evidence gathering, and they were welcome to go to the airport. She also returned Helen's cooking DVD.

As she handed it to him, Thomas thanked her, and he felt the now-familiar sweep of wings down the sides of his stomach. What would happen when Dave decided to take flight, he wondered.

Mr. Moran and Aunt Sadie organized a volunteer search for the following day, when other freshman composition teachers from the community college where his father taught, people from the bank where Aunt Sadie worked, members of their church, and Helen's friends from the day-care center would most likely be available.

The morning of the search it snowed.

"She'll leave footprints," Thomas said, looking out the kitchen window at the birdbath, its rim sprinkled with snow.

"Yes." Aunt Sadie pulled him close to her.

"It's quite possible," his father murmured. "Anything is possible." His father hadn't shaved. He hadn't slept.

"I need to collect a few things from home and water my plants," Aunt Sadie said as Thomas clung to her. "And then I'll meet you at the airport, Brian, and—" Aunt Sadie broke off, staring at Thomas's father. "You need to take a shower. Remember, Theresa is bringing Martin over. She's going to watch the boys while we're with the search team."

Thomas sat in his chair at the kitchen table, waiting for Martin. His father was in the shower when his phone rang. Thomas watched it glow on the table. Then he picked it up and pressed the green button.

"Hello?" he said.

"Is this the Moran residence?"

"Yes."

"Helen's home?"

"Yes." Thomas pressed the phone to his ear.

"I believe I can help you find your wife, Mr. Moran."

Thomas remained silent. It wasn't right to pretend to be someone you weren't.

"I'm not talking about a physical search. My name is Marina Rush. I'm a clairvoyant. It is possible she's trying to contact you even now. Give you clues. With your permission, I'll consult the astral plane."

"Is she . . . cold?" Thomas asked. "She took her dress coat, not the down one, and she wasn't wearing her winter boots."

"Is this a child? I need to speak to Mr. Moran."

Thomas heard his father's steps in the hallway and felt what he presumed were the little hairs on the bottom of Dave's feet crawling up the side of his stomach. He pressed the red button and placed the phone upside down on the table.

"I finished book four of the *Galaxies Dawn*," Martin said, handing the book to Thomas. "Is book five still checked out, do you know?" Thomas took the book from Martin. They'd been trading the series back and forth since there was only one copy of each book in the school library and it didn't take them three weeks to finish. Now he had trouble remembering what the story was about.

"I don't know," he said.

Mrs. Templeton made them lunch, and afterward Martin asked, "Do you want to play Chinese checkers?" Chinese checkers was his favorite board game.

Thomas nodded. He knew that the game would keep Martin busy reviewing all his available moves while trying to build a strategic bridge. With Mrs. Templeton clearing out the fridge and washing dishes, this left Thomas free to think his own thoughts.

He'd stopped asking Martin how many seconds his mother had been missing. This morning, he'd been wondering if Helen might have amnesia.

"Maybe she hit her head," he said to Martin as his friend hopped across the game board.

"Maybe," Martin said.

In the middle of their third game, Aunt Sadie arrived. She walked through the side door with her briefcase and her overnight bag; she didn't need to tell Thomas and Martin and Mrs. Templeton they hadn't found Helen.

"I was thinking that maybe she hit her head," Thomas whispered to Aunt Sadie after they'd said their good-byes to the Templetons. "That she has amnesia."

"That's why we're looking so hard for her, Duck." She squeezed his shoulders before sitting down next to him and taking his hand. They sat together in silence until Aunt Sadie decided to go outside and put salt on the front walk.

It was almost evening when Thomas's father came home carrying a bundle of something. He came in the front door, sat on a stair, and laid his head on the bundle.

Thomas closed the door. In only six days he'd grown used to his father breaking all the rules they'd kept so strictly since Thomas could remember.

Mr. Moran looked up, noticed Thomas, and asked him to get his aunt.

When they both stood in front of him on the stair, Thomas's father unrolled the bundle: "It's Helen's coat. We found it after you left."

Aunt Sadie reached out for it. "But how—"

"It was hanging in a tree, which is probably why no one saw it before. It's the same brown color as the bark." Mr. Moran wouldn't let go of the coat, but he held it up. "It must have been too cold for the dogs to find it."

Thomas moved closer. He sniffed. It didn't smell like his mother—it smelled cold.

"I'll hang it in the closet," Aunt Sadie said, once again holding out her hands.

"No! There's more, but—" Mr. Moran glanced at Thomas and Thomas knew not to look away. He was good at staring contests with his mother. He could always go longer than she could without blinking. It was harder to stare at his father, but Thomas knew somehow if he didn't do it, that his father wouldn't reveal the more that Thomas felt he had to know.

"Thomas, go to your room, please."

Aunt Sadie moved to block Thomas's path. "We agreed, Brian. I don't want him to hear whatever you have to say from anyone else."

Thomas's father rubbed at his eyes beneath his glasses. "The truth of the matter is, we haven't the faintest idea what has happened to your mother, Thomas."

"I don't think she's at that airport anymore," Thomas said. "She's . . . gone somewhere else."

Mr. Moran stood up. Thomas sat in the place his father had vacated. Thomas's mouth was suddenly dry and Dave seemed to be trying a downward takeoff. For some reason, Thomas thought of Chef Philippe: *Here we go.*

"Son," Mr. Moran began.

Thomas stood up. Aunt Sadie slipped her hand into his and squeezed it tight as they waited for his father to speak.

"I don't want to say this out loud." Thomas's father was looking at Thomas, not his aunt.

Thomas took a step back, pressing his head into Aunt Sadie's ribs. Her arms closed around him.

"After so many days . . . in temperatures that have fallen below freezing. And without this." Mr. Moran held up Helen's coat in his clenched fists. "Officer Grant said the police are changing the classification of the search from missing person to, well . . ."

He couldn't look at his son and finish his sentence. "One of recovery. Your mother couldn't survive outside this long in these temperatures. What we're trying to do now is find her body."

Thomas broke Aunt Sadie's hold to free his arms. He pointed at his father. "Why don't you ever listen to me? I *told* you, you haven't found her yet because she's somewhere else."

"I agree with Thomas," Aunt Sadie said. "She's not there. If she were...I'd...I think I would have felt something. But, Thomas—" Aunt Sadie spun Thomas around. "I'm not saying that to give you false hope." She pulled him to her and Thomas felt...crushed. Then, leaning back so that she could look him in the eyes, she said, "I don't think she's anywhere."

Chapter 15

That night, Mrs. Sharp sat once again beside Thomas's bed while his aunt and his father met with Detective Freeman at the police station about "next steps." Mrs. Sharp's knitting needles clicked on in such a regular pattern that it reminded Thomas of a toy train.

The ball of yarn rolled off her lap and she made an "oof" noise as she bent to retrieve it. She placed the ball in Thomas's hands. "Would you hold this, Thomas?"

He sat up. The ball was light, like there was air at the center.

"I was wondering—" Thomas broke off, considering whether he wanted to know the answer to the question he was about to ask.

"Don't hold so tight, dear." Mrs. Sharp traced the strand from Thomas's hands to her knitting, tugging gently as she did so. "Let go a little. That's right. Now you're the perfect spindle."

Thomas had to work to stay relaxed. He had never held a ball and let it go at the same time. He took a deep breath and willed Dave to fold up his wings so they weren't covering his airway. "Do you think my mother is dead?" he asked finally.

Mrs. Sharp put her hand on Thomas's knee. "I hope not," she said, "but it is a possibility. I am so sorry, Thomas."

Mrs. Sharp resumed her knitting and they were silent for a while, Thomas concentrating on the pull of the yarn between his fingers.

"Aunt Sadie says that my mother isn't anywhere. But she must be somewhere."

"I have an idea," Mrs. Sharp said. "Why don't we imagine a place for Helen?"

"My father says—"

"Your father likes facts. But since we don't have all the facts, we could make some up. That is, if you'd like."

Thomas thought about informing Mrs. Sharp that you couldn't *make up* facts. But he realized in the same moment that he very much wanted to. So he nodded.

"Would it be warm?" he asked Mrs. Sharp.

"Warm . . . like the desert?"

No.

Thomas did not think his mother was in the desert. "Would *she* be warm?"

"Oh yes. Absolutely."

"Would there be . . . magic?"

"I don't see why not. It's your story."

Thomas nodded. Helen liked stories with magic.

"And talking animals?"

Mrs. Sharp nodded again. "Talking animals are very common in invented places."

"Yes. And it has to be cozy. Like...inside a blanket...or a big coat."

"All right, then," she said. "Close your eyes and see if this feels right."

Thomas closed his eyes and concentrated on the soft yarn at the tips of his fingers.

"Helen drove to the airport and parked her car," Mrs. Sharp said. "She sat there for a long time, looking out the window."

"What was she thinking?" Thomas asked, his eyes still pressed closed, hoping for a glimpse of his mother.

"About you, of course. And your father. And your aunt. Then, all of a sudden, it began to snow."

"But it didn't snow on the first day."

"Hmm, yes that's so. But maybe this was magical snow... meant only for Helen. You did want magic, didn't you?"

"Right," Thomas replied. "Yes to magic."

"The snow fell thick and soft, until...until there was a quilt of snow. Helen sat inside the car looking at it with wonder."

"Was she sad? Were the clouds in her eyes?" Thomas felt a tug on the yarn and he reminded himself to loosen his grip.

"Yes...and no. She was sad to be leaving, but she was also

about to take a journey, one she knew only she could take. She was...determined. Something was calling to her, Thomas. Listen." Mrs. Sharp made a shushing sound. "Do you hear that?"

"No." Thomas heard nothing; but he felt the soft snow falling and drifting up against the car, silent and warm, like... a thousand balls of yarn.

"I'm quite sure I hear something. I'll wait until you can hear it, too. Relax, Thomas. It will come to you."

It took some time, but Thomas thought *maybe* he did hear something. "Someone's knocking," he said, listening harder to make sure. "On the car door."

"Yes, that's it. And now that someone is wiping away the snow from Helen's window."

"It's a mitten," Thomas said. "Or...a great big paw."

"A paw. Yes. I thought so, too."

At the thought of his mother in the car like that—all alone—Thomas felt Dave's wings brush the top of his stomach. He took a deep breath and let it out. Slowly. One more breath. Then another.

"I think I see a snout. Do you?" Mrs. Sharp asked him.

He *did* see it...emerging from the blankness. "A polar bear," he said. "White like the snow."

"Yes," Mrs. Sharp agreed. "His paw beckons to Helen and she gets out of the car."

Once again, Thomas squeezed the ball of yarn and felt

the tug of Mrs. Sharp's knitting needles. "The bear won't hurt her," he said with certainty.

"No. He wants to help."

Thomas peeked at Mrs. Sharp before squeezing his eyes shut again. "I don't hear anything, do you?"

"No."

"Why aren't they talking?" Thomas tried to get a clear view of the bear, but the snow kept covering him up. "The bear is sad," Thomas said after a moment. "The clouds are in *his* eyes."

"Something must be troubling him. But he's not ready—or maybe he can't... share it yet. Helen stands quite still, looking into the bear's eyes."

Thomas nodded his head. "She's good at being patient."

"The snow continues falling," Mrs. Sharp resumed. "Soon it covers her shoulders, her hair, even her eyelashes. She shivers a little. The bear gestures again, this time for her to follow him to a clearing where the tree cover is so heavy the snow has piled up on the branches. It's... more like a cave. Helen watches as the bear turns over a rock and produces a fur coat from underneath it."

"Oh no. It can't be fur." Thomas was quite sure on this point. "She wouldn't like that. She wouldn't even wear the coat Aunt Sadie found for her at New-4-U, the one with the fur trim on the hood."

"Of course she wouldn't. This is a magic coat, Thomas. It's the coat of the very first polar bear queen. She died long ago, but her coat stayed behind to . . . protect travelers. Travelers like Helen. It has been passed down for hundreds of years."

"Well then . . . that's different." Thomas paused, thinking. "And she needs a coat. She took hers off."

"Yes, I know. Your father told me. Shall we continue?"

Thomas nodded.

"Helen takes off her coat and hangs it in the branches. The polar bear helps her on with the fur coat and as she puts her arms in the sleeves, this terrible heaviness she's felt these last couple of years . . . it's beginning to feel . . ."

"Lighter," Thomas said. He handed the ball of yarn back to Mrs. Sharp and turned over on his stomach, letting one arm dangle over the side of the bed. His bed was so high that his fingers didn't reach the floor. He wiggled them, thinking. "Her shoes aren't warm enough, either," he said.

The knitting needles paused in their rhythmic clicking and Thomas saw that Mrs. Sharp was staring out the window that overlooked the backyard.

"Something is happening inside Helen," she said finally. "She's feeling a great warm surge of energy. The bear sweeps his paw to indicate her feet."

"I still don't understand why he doesn't talk to her."

"Only you know that, Thomas."

"But I don't." It bothered Thomas. In a magical story, the bear *should* talk. "Maybe the bear is under a spell," he told Mrs. Sharp. "Keep going."

"From underneath the same rock," Mrs. Sharp continued,

"the bear produces a pair of boots, thick and sturdy and warm. Does this sound right to you, Thomas?"

Thomas nodded. "They were left behind, too, to protect travelers like my mother," he murmured.

"Helen sits down on the rock, takes off her shoes, and—"

"Pulls them on," Thomas interrupted Mrs. Sharp. He couldn't help it. He wanted her to know that he was seeing it, too.

There was a moment of silence as Thomas and Mrs. Sharp looked at each other. It was as if they'd come to a place in the road where they could turn left or right and each wanted the other to say which way.

"We're coming up to it," he said.

"Coming up to what?"

"The part where the polar bear talks. He *is* under a spell; he can only talk this one time." Thomas asked himself, what would a sad bear say to his mother? He wanted the bear to tell her to turn around, get back in the car, and go home. But he knew that wasn't what the bear was going to say.

"You're about to set off on a journey, Helen..." Mrs. Sharp said, speaking in a low voice that didn't sound much like a polar bear. Turning so he faced the wall, Thomas pulled his pillow over his head and closed his eyes. He lay quiet, breathing in and out, imagining his story.

"Are you frightened?" said the polar bear.
Helen shook her head.

"Only you can do this," he said, reaching deep down under the rock and pulling out a bag with a long, thin cord. *"Here. You will need this on your journey."*

The scene disappeared from view and Thomas sat up. He looked at Mrs. Sharp and blinked. "He gave her a bag," he said. "It has a long cord and she put it around her neck and tucked it inside her coat."

"What is in the bag?" Mrs. Sharp asked.

Thomas shook his head. He didn't know. He lay back down and looked at the ceiling. There was a curved crack above his head. As Thomas stared at it, he imagined that the ceiling was a field of snow and he was looking down on it, searching until he found his mother and the bear.

The bear turned away from Helen and closed his mouth around his claw, like Dave sucking on a finger. But he wasn't sucking on it. He pulled it from his paw. There was a drop of blood on the end of it, where he'd torn it away.

"Why would he do that?" he asked aloud. "Is he giving it to her?"

"Giving her what, Thomas? My sight isn't as good as yours."

"His claw. He pulled it right out of his paw. And now he's..." Thomas paused, his gaze fixed on the ceiling.

"Here's a whistle," he said as he folded it into her palm. "I would give my life to save you, Helen. You know this. Use it to call me—but remember, the whistle can only be used once."

The great white bear blew into the claw until it doubled in size. It was a whistle with an opening where it should have been attached to his paw and two small holes along its sharp, curved length. Before he turned back to Helen, he licked the blood away.

Thomas relayed to Mrs. Sharp what had happened and she said, "I'm guessing Helen took the whistle and placed it in the bag she'd hidden beneath her coat."

Thomas nodded. "It's not the only thing in the bag..." He could see something else, something round and soft, but he didn't know what yet.

Thomas waited. But nothing more came to him.

"It's time for her to leave, isn't it?" Thomas asked Mrs. Sharp.

"Yes, I believe it is time for Helen to say good-bye to the bear."

"Maybe she's going to the astral plane."

"How do you know about the astral plane?" Mrs. Sharp paused in her knitting to look at Thomas.

It was easy for him to tell her about the phone call. And Marina Rush. And the astral plane. She wouldn't mind that Thomas had answered the phone while his father was in the shower.

"She said if I wanted her to, she would search for my mother there."

For some reason, Mrs. Sharp began to knit faster. Tap. Tap. Tap. "Easy for her to say, since the astral plane cannot be seen."

"Then how do we know it's real?"

"We don't, but I believe the astral plane was considered by classical scholars to be a place between the world of the living and the world of the dead. Is that where you'd like your mother to go in your story?"

Thomas was still, trying to decide if the astral plane was a good place for Helen to go. "Can the astral plane be more north than north and more south than south?" Thomas asked, remembering a fairy tale he and his mother had liked to read.

"I don't see why not."

"Then yes. She's going to the astral plane now."

"Helen is stroking the polar bear's soft white neck," Mrs. Sharp said after some time. " 'Thank you,' she is saying. 'Thank you more than I can say.' He bends down toward her as if he is about to whisper something in her ear. But all Helen feels is his fur brushing against her face."

"Like butterfly kisses," Thomas murmured, thinking of the times his mother brushed her eyelashes against his face.

"Yes. Almost like a kiss. As she turns to get her bearings and find the horizon, a great gust of wind knocks drifts of snow from the branches above and they swirl around Helen. When she turns back toward the bear, he is gone."

Thomas pressed his lips together and swallowed. "How—"

He rubbed his eyes with his fists to keep the tears inside. "How can a story start with good-bye?"

"I don't know," Mrs. Sharp told him. "But you do. Somewhere inside you know the answer."

"So it's . . . not over?"

"No . . . no! It's only just begun. At least you can rest easy now knowing that wherever Helen is, she is perfectly warm, Thomas. We are agreed on that point, are we not?"

Thomas nodded.

"And somewhere in this house you are going to re-create the safe warm feeling Helen has inside her coat. Maybe right here, under your covers. When you go there, you will imagine what is happening in the story. And then you will discover what comes next. Do you understand, Thomas?"

Thomas nodded. He rolled over to face the wall again and pulled his knees up close, snuggling under the covers with every intention of spinning out more of the story, but all he could do was picture his mother in her coat of fur and her sturdy boots, as if she were inside a snow globe, slowly disappearing behind a curtain of snow.

He slept deeply for the first time in days, knowing she was warm.

Chapter 16

It was not in his bed, but underneath it where Thomas would go to think about his story. He had created a space for himself there after Baby Sadie died. He went there when his mother retreated to her room and closed the curtains. Thomas called it UnderLand. His father didn't like it when he tucked himself beneath the bed behind the sweater boxes since that made Thomas hard to find; but his father wasn't *always* the boss of him.

After school the next day, Thomas got his mother's wool coat from the closet and, pulling aside the boxes, spread the coat out like a blanket and pushed it up against the wall. He slid on top of it and pulled the boxes back into place before wrapping himself in a layer of wool. Closing his eyes, he lay still, thinking about his mother and the sad polar bear.

"I like this," Dave said.

Thomas opened his eyes. His butterfly was talking. For

some reason, he thought of Mrs. Evans's explanation about the stomach being the second brain. Inside his stomach, Dave's wings opened and closed as if approving of the thought.

His father was calling. "Come down, Thomas! You have a visitor."

Scattering the boxes, Thomas slid out from under the bed. He ran downstairs feeling as if he'd been caught doing something he wasn't supposed to do.

"Thomas!" Giselle enveloped him in her big puffy jacket, pressing her cheek against his, her lips kissing the air. "Êtes-vous bien? Are you well?" She pushed him away to regard him at arm's length. "That's a silly question, isn't it, bien sûr que non. Of course you're not. I've brought you some chocolate madeleines. There's a lady at the bakery who speaks French to me if there are no customers."

"Why don't you come in, Giselle?" Thomas's father said.

"Merci, Monsieur Moran."

"You can eat the cookies in the kitchen," his father said, before returning to his office in the basement.

Thomas and Giselle went into the kitchen. Every surface was covered with unfamiliar packages: baskets of fruit they hadn't purchased, tins of nuts, and Thomas knew that the freezer was filled with casserole dishes with masking tape labels in unfamiliar handwriting. Where had it all come from?

Giselle took off her jacket, sat down at the table, untied the box, and bit into a cookie. Using her pinkie to sweep the crumbs into her other hand, she said: "Go on. Tell me. You have a secret. I can tell by your posture. And the way you keep rubbing the side of your face."

Thomas joined her at the table and nodded. It was the best secret he'd ever had.

My mother is warm!

She was protected inside the polar bear's coat and boots. She could curl up and sleep on the snow if she needed to. Polar bears did that and they stayed snug and dry.

"If I tell you, it won't be a secret," Thomas said, tracing his finger along the edge of the table.

"Of course it will. That's why people say they'll *let you in* on the secret. It's like inviting you into their fort. Once we're inside together, we close the door. Then it's *our* secret."

While she was talking, Giselle placed her hand on Thomas's. Did she know that Thomas had a fort? No. She couldn't possibly know about UnderLand.

Her hand was so warm.

"My mother's in a story," he said. "Mrs. Sharp and I put her there last night."

"You mean . . . like a fairy tale?" Giselle asked in a whisper, scooting her chair closer to Thomas. "A 'Once upon a time . . . happily ever after' fairy tale?"

"We only have 'Once upon a time,' " he said. "So far. She met a polar bear."

"A polar bear," Giselle repeated.

Taking the cookie Giselle handed him, Thomas nibbled

at it to please her. It tasted like sand. He didn't know why, but everything he ate tasted like sand…or oatmeal. Watery oatmeal, the way his father made it. "Mrs. Sharp helped me begin," he said. "The polar bear gave my mother a coat handed down from the very first polar bear queen. She had to get warm. First things first."

"Thomas?" Giselle asked, squeezing his hand. "Can I play, too?"

Before Thomas could answer, she finished her cookie and said, "I just had an idea. I'll be right back."

And then all that occupied the kitchen besides himself and the fruit baskets and the tins of nuts was the sound of the front door slamming. He wondered if telling Giselle had been a good idea.

"Nope." Dave weighed in, fluttering his wings for no reason at all.

When Giselle returned, she placed a fabric bag on the table with a clunk. Covered in lions—the kind that stood up on flags and coats of arms—the bag was lined with scarlet fabric and cinched tight with a gold cord. Thomas could tell this was not an ordinary bag.

Pushing the bag over to Thomas, Giselle extracted another cookie from the box. "Go on," she said, biting into her madeleine. "Open it."

Thomas worked at the knot until it loosened. He reached in and pulled out a shiny coin with a rooster on one side and a man with leaves in his hair on the other.

"They're all different." Reaching into the bag, Giselle sifted through the coins. "There's one I especially like—here it is!" She handed Thomas a silver coin with the figure of a woman in a long dress, her face turned away. "It reminds me of your mother."

Thomas brought the coin closer to his face. Even stamped onto silver, this woman seemed to have more energy than his mother. She was going somewhere, walking so quickly that her hair could not keep up.

"What are these?" he asked Giselle.

"Francs," she replied. "They don't use them in France anymore. They've used euros since 1999. My mom helps me collect them. But I want to donate them now. To the story. A sack of shiny gold and silver coins can come in very handy in a fairy tale."

While Giselle talked, Thomas rolled a little bite of madeleine around in his mouth.

Did money exist in the astral plane? If it did, and his mother needed to pay for shelter for the night or a loaf of bread, these shiny coins seemed more useful than the credit cards she'd left behind.

"But how...how will we get them to her?" he asked Giselle.

"I don't know. Maybe by making a wish." Giselle's hand hovered over the cookie box. "Thomas, you need to finish at least one cookie. They're quite small, really."

Chapter 17

It was Friday the thirteenth. After school, Thomas sat at the kitchen table across from his father, who was fumbling with the wrapper on a package of graham crackers. They ate their crackers without plates, sprinkling crumbs on the table.

"Mrs. Sharp called earlier," his father told Thomas. "She needs your help in the kitchen . . . There's a jar she can't open. It's just as well. I have a manuscript I need to finish copyediting. I've fallen so far behind."

Mrs. Sharp had told Thomas that his father was a concrete thinker, so they must come up with something concrete for Thomas to do at her house so that he could come over. This was just a little help—not like the job she'd suggested before that Mr. Moran had decided was not appropriate for Thomas while he was in school and had homework.

After the crumbs had been swept off the table, Thomas left for Mrs. Sharp's house. He had mentioned to her that

Giselle wanted to help with the story, so she'd invited her as well.

Thomas didn't have to ring the bell because Mrs. Sharp said she'd leave the front door unlocked and he could let himself in. Just inside, there was an alcove where he sat to take off his boots and coat, and beyond that, a glass door made of nine panels, each painted with a flower the size of Thomas's head. He pressed his nose to the glass and could see around the flowers a glimpse of Mrs. Sharp's living room: a bookcase, flames in the fireplace, a patch of maroon velvet armchair.

"Thomas, why do you stand out there looking in?" Mrs. Sharp asked as she opened the glass door. "Come and sit by the fire. I'll get us some tea."

Thomas sat on a low footstool by the fire, looking at the pictures on the rug that covered up most of the floor. In the center, a woman and a man were taking a walk. She had on a long dress and he wore a funny coat Thomas recognized from books he'd seen about castles. She was smiling, her hand resting on the man's arm. In one corner, hunters set off with dogs; in another, boys kicked a ball to one another. Sun shone on the couple in the center of the rug. Behind them was a dark forest. Through a clearing, you could see in the distance a range of snowcapped mountains. This scene was surrounded by a border of smaller pictures of strange-looking plants and flowers.

"Am I late?" Giselle was peeling off her jacket as she opened the alcove door. She sat on the bench, kicked off her boots, and closed the door behind her before taking a seat in the velvet armchair.

"I'm just making tea," Mrs. Sharp called from the kitchen.

Mrs. Sharp returned, setting a tray crowded with canisters of all kinds, teacups, and a china teapot down on her coffee table. "One of life's great luxuries is a fine selection of teas," she said, taking her place on the couch. "Giselle, I think you would enjoy this spicy plum, but you can choose whatever one you like." As Thomas considered his choices, Mrs. Sharp pointed to a container. "Would you like to try Helen's favorite?"

Taking the cylinder she offered, Thomas twisted off the lid. For a moment he was in their herb garden, overwhelmed by the scent of peppermint leaves. And something else... something lemony. He could see his mother beside him. In the garden. She wore her pink sweater; she was bending over and picking something.

"Thomas." Giselle tugged on his arm. "Where did you go just now? You had the strangest look on your face."

Thomas blinked. "I saw my mother," he told them. "She was picking lemon balm in our garden."

"That's a sense memory," Mrs. Sharp said as Thomas dropped his tea bag into the cup she offered. "They're lovely, aren't they?"

Pressing her fingers against the lid of the teapot, she filled Thomas's teacup with water. Thomas held the cup in its saucer on his lap, letting the steam and the scent of herbs float up to his nose.

"Oh, dear. I almost forgot," said Mrs. Sharp. She went back into the kitchen and brought out a jar of jam. "I couldn't put this on my breakfast toast this morning. Will you unscrew it for me?"

Thomas was used to opening jars; he had to use the tail of his shirt on this one, it was so tight.

"Thank you." Mrs. Sharp set the jar down at her side. "Now." Rubbing her hands together, Mrs. Sharp said to Thomas, "I think today we need to discover what Helen's quest will be. Every hero has a quest."

"And every heroine," Giselle added, pinching her tea bag and dropping it on her saucer. "Did you bring the coins I gave you, Thomas?"

Thomas stood and went to get the coins out of his coat pocket, feeling his uncertainty about them, as lumpy and heavy as the bag itself. He thumped it onto the table by the tray.

"I have just the place for that." Mrs. Sharp drew out a chain from underneath her collar and unfastened the key that dangled from it. Then she went over to her rolltop desk and, from the bottom drawer, pulled out a tarnished metal box. The key fit neatly in the lock. With one twist it sprung open on a well-oiled hinge.

"How old is this?" Giselle asked, running her finger over the dented surface.

"There's no saying. My mother kept her valuables in it during the war and hid it under the floorboards. There wasn't much, but with enemy soldiers everywhere. . . . This," she said, pointing to the ring on her finger, "she kept this in there and wore a cheap metal band instead. But it's been empty for quite some time now." Mrs. Sharp pushed the box toward Thomas. "I think it belongs to you now. Keep it somewhere safe."

Giselle transferred the bag of coins to the box and pressed the lid back down.

"Thank you," Thomas said, taking the key out of the lock and putting it in his pocket. He knew just where the box belonged—behind the sweater boxes in UnderLand, where he'd stowed his mother's coat and the cooking DVD of Chef Philippe that Officer Grant had returned to them. "I will take good care of it."

"Of course you will. Now, we know that Helen is about to start on a journey. But why?"

"Maybe she's looking for something," Giselle suggested.

"Or maybe someone." Mrs. Sharp looked at Thomas as though she knew he'd be the next to speak.

"Sadie," he whispered.

"Your aunt?" Giselle asked.

"No," said Thomas.

"The baby Helen lost," Mrs. Sharp said quietly.

"Oh . . . right." Giselle lowered her gaze and sipped her tea. "My mom told me about that."

Other people said Helen lost the baby, too; but she hadn't really. "Baby Sadie is not lost," Thomas told them. He knew exactly where she was. Behind the church. In the cemetery.

"But she's lost to you and to your mother and father," Mrs. Sharp said. "In a manner of speaking. So she could be lost in your story."

"That's true." Thomas stared into the fire. "Maybe she set off on her journey to find Baby Sadie and bring her home. Do you think the polar bear queen might help her?"

"I think the polar bear queen is a natural choice," Mrs. Sharp agreed. "But how will Helen find her to ask for help?"

Thomas didn't know. "She lives far away," he said.

"She lives in a castle made of ice," Giselle said. "And she has funny footmen... Maybe they're penguins, who—"

"No!" That didn't seem right at all to Thomas. There were no funny penguins in his story. It was serious.

"You have to let Thomas lead us, Giselle. It is his story."

"How do we do that?" Giselle asked, fingering the tassel that dangled from the arm of her chair.

"By asking questions. To help draw the story out of him."

Giselle turned to Thomas. "How will your mom find the polar bear queen? Will the polar bear take her? The one who gave her the coat?"

"No," Thomas said. "They said good-bye." What a strange feeling he was having. He didn't know how he knew, but he knew. He wasn't trying to make it up. The ideas were already there, like looking for your socks under the covers. You knew they were there, you just didn't know where.

"And where is Helen now, Thomas?" Mrs. Sharp asked, setting her cup in her saucer and placing it on the table.

Thomas shook his head, waiting. He closed his eyes. There was so much snow. It swirled everywhere, wrapping his mother in a powdery softness. "She started her journey, but now...she's lost," he told them. "In a snowstorm."

Thomas heard Giselle's voice. "Can you see her? Will you help her find the way to the queen's castle?"

Thomas shook his head again. He wasn't even sure polar bear queens lived in castles. If only Giselle would stop talking.

He wanted so much to be alone with his mother.

Chapter 18

Mrs. Evans was now so big that the children had to re-arrange their desks to make the center aisle wide enough for her to pass through. Martin thought it had more to do with the increasing amount of Nilla wafers she ate while the students did their sustained silent reading than her pregnancy. He brought up the subject again on Monday afternoon during recess, which, due to the icy weather conditions, the children were having in the gym. "She's eating so many it's enough to make a line item in the Evanses' family budget," Martin told Thomas, kicking back the basketball George repeatedly let slip from his fingers to sail in their direction.

At Thomas's father's suggestion, Martin's parents had introduced him to the concept of budgeting to see if his counting could be turned into a useful skill.

"How long has it been?" Thomas asked, stopping the basketball once again and trapping it under his foot.

Though it had been some time since he'd asked, Martin knew exactly what Thomas was talking about. "Hours? Minutes?"

"Days. Hours." Thomas hesitated. "Minutes, but not seconds."

"Throw me the basketball, turd," George called.

"Thirteen days, twenty-three hours, and seventeen minutes."

"How long can you be outside in freezing temperatures before you—" Thomas could not finish the sentence.

Dave poked Thomas with his proboscis. He was not pleased.

Thomas had never asked Martin this question before, but he suspected his friend had done the math.

"There are too many variables. I can't give you an accurate answer."

Thomas stared at Martin. Why was it so easy to look him in the eyes, Thomas wondered. Because they were best friends? Or because when Martin looked back, Thomas knew he wasn't searching for the usual things that everyone else seemed to be searching for—like how Thomas was holding up.

"I said give me that basketball. I signed out number twelve. It's mine." George was advancing.

"Be conservative," Thomas said. "In hours, please." Thomas picked up the ball. He turned it so that he could see the number 12 on it.

"Seventeen."

"Are you deaf? I'll tell Mrs. Evans if you don't hand it over."

"George Panagopoulos has a broken nose?" Mr. Moran was sitting in Mrs. Evans's classroom across the desk from Thomas's teacher and Principal Bowen. Both he and Mrs. Templeton had been called in after school to discuss the incident at recess.

"His glasses certainly," Mrs. Evans said. "They won't know about his nose until they see the specialist this afternoon."

"It was just a bad pass," Martin said. "Thomas didn't mean to hit him in the face."

"It serves George right." Mrs. Templeton slapped her gloves on Mrs. Evans's desk. "I can say that privately, can't I, Principal Bowen? George Panagopoulos is a bully. He's always picking on Martin."

Principal Bowen did not respond to Mrs. Templeton. Instead, she turned to Thomas: "Did you intend to hurt George when you returned his ball?"

This, of course, was the million-dollar question.

"I . . . don't know. It just . . . happened."

"That is not an acceptable answer, Thomas," Mr. Moran said. "You either did or you didn't."

"I think we should ask George why the ball was in Thomas's possession in the first place," Mrs. Templeton said. "Martin, were you and Thomas playing basketball with George?"

Martin shook his head. "No. And I think George was—"

He broke off and glanced at Thomas. "George was playing dodgeball."

"With a *basketball*? I see. Did George try to hit you with the ball?"

"Yes."

"How many times?"

"Seven."

"Seven times before the incident occurred. Why is it, I wonder, that George's behavior went unnoticed, Mrs. Evans?"

Mrs. Evans explained patiently that due to the icy conditions, they had held indoor recess in the gymnasium with just one monitor for twenty-eight children. It was impossible to track each and every movement.

"Well, there you have it." Sitting back and making a clucking noise with her tongue, Mrs. Templeton got ready to rest her case. "If the best predictor of future behavior is past behavior and Thomas and Martin have never lifted a finger against anyone in the classroom and George's record is populated with skirmishes, then I see no need to question Thomas further."

Thomas's father had been holding up his hand since the beginning of Mrs. Templeton's speech, and when she finished, he said: "If you please, Theresa, I'd like to get to the bottom of this."

"You really are quite clueless, aren't you, Brian?" Martin's mother replied. "Do you have any idea what happens here at school? Do you know, for example, that Helen forgot to add sugar to the cupcakes she baked for Thomas's birthday last April and that George called Thomas, Son of the Space Cadet?"

Mrs. Templeton took a deep breath as if gathering energy to continue her speech.

"That's quite enough for one day, Theresa. Thank you," Principal Bowen said. She stood up, indicating that the meeting was over. "I will tell Mrs. Panagopoulos that, after speaking with you and the boys, I've determined the incident was an accident. Since Thomas has already apologized, we will consider the matter closed."

"You can tell Mrs. Panagopoulos from me that if George so much as approaches Martin or Thomas to tease or belittle them—"

"Mom." Martin tugged on his mother's sleeve. Mrs. Templeton was wound up like an eight-day clock, as Aunt Sadie liked to say.

Brushing at her eye with one hand and placing the other on Thomas's head, she took a deep breath to calm down. "I'm sorry, Thomas. I just don't want to see you hurt anymore, sweetie."

"Thank you for your concern, Theresa, but it's misplaced." Mr. Moran took Martin's hand and stood up. "We're doing fine."

The rest of the room waited for him to realize that he'd grabbed the wrong boy.

Dropping Martin's hand, Mr. Moran said with emphasis: "Thomas and I are doing fine."

Chapter 19

"You're so cold, Thomas," Mrs. Sharp said as she clasped his hands the following afternoon. She'd called Mr. Moran to see if Thomas could help her bring in some firewood, and since Aunt Sadie was too busy at the bank to watch him as she usually did on Tuesdays, Mr. Moran had said yes. If he thought it odd that Mrs. Sharp suddenly needed help, he hadn't mentioned it.

"Sit here by the fire." Taking a velvet floor cushion, she set it down on the rug near the fireplace. Giselle made him a cup of lemon balm tea and placed it on the bricks in front of the grate.

While Giselle told Mrs. Sharp about her day at school and determined whether there was anise in the little cookies on the table, Thomas let his finger travel to an image on the rug he hadn't seen before—an animal half hidden in the bushes at the edge of the woods. The light from the fire moved over the rug, making it seem as if a breeze was blowing through the forest that hid the creature. Thomas leaned in so he could see the whole picture. That's when he realized it was a little fox, with one paw caught tight in a trap. The rug maker had chosen to capture the fox in that moment of agonizing pain, twisting violently to get away.

"No." Thomas sat up.

"Thomas? What is it?" Mrs. Sharp set down her cup and started from her chair.

"Nothing. I . . . The fox," was all he managed to say.

"Oh." She sat back down. "Poor creature."

"The fox?" Giselle said. "What are you talking about, Thomas?"

"I try to keep him tucked under the footstool, but every once in a while someone discovers the poor thing."

As Mrs. Sharp spoke, Giselle got down on her hands and knees to see what had startled Thomas. He knelt next to her.

"Is that a . . . Oh, that's awful! He's in such pain." Giselle sat back. "It's just . . . he's frozen there. He's *always* going to have his paw in that trap."

"Think of it as an illustration in a book, Giselle," Mrs. Sharp said. "How many illustrations have you seen of Snow White sleeping in the casket after she ate the poison apple? But you know very well that's not how the story ends."

"But this isn't a book. It's a rug!"

"I know. And not every story has a happy ending, though I would like to imagine another ending for this little fox."

Moving over to the fire, Mrs. Sharp repositioned the footstool so that the injured fox was covered up again. "But that's not why we're here, so let's return to Helen. When we last left her, she was lost in a snowstorm."

Thomas reached for his teacup, but the image wouldn't leave him. "Maybe..." he began. "What if she comes upon the fox in the woods?"

"Ooh, I like that," Giselle said. "And rescues him."

"Think very carefully about that, Thomas," Mrs. Sharp said. "Not everything can be saved."

He knew that. Thomas heard his father's voice telling him the fox was not his concern. "Everyone has problems, Thomas. It's enough to take care of your own."

Setting his cup on the bricks, Thomas closed his eyes, trying to erase the fox and invite the snow back in. He waited until snow was swirling all around him, until he could feel the flakes stinging his cheek.

"She's been walking for hours," he said. "She's tired."

"Where is she?" he heard Giselle ask.

"In the woods. It's dark, but the snow has stopped and... there's a moon." Thomas saw a sliver of light slicing through the trees. "Not a full moon."

"Is Helen frightened?" Mrs. Sharp was talking now.

Thomas had to concentrate even harder to know what his mother was feeling. Pressing his cheek to his knees, he grabbed the fabric of his pants at his ankles, holding tight.

"You needn't work so hard, Thomas. Try to relax."

Taking a deep breath, Thomas imagined an icy wind stinging his cheeks.

Relax! Relax.

Nothing.

A black curtain had fallen in front of the scene. Like the end of a play. He curled up on the floor, letting the fire warm his back. He lay there for a long time, or so it seemed.

Then he felt a poke in his stomach. "Yes," Dave said. "She is afraid."

"A little afraid," Thomas said aloud. He returned to his breath and to the black curtain and resolved to wait until something—anything—appeared. Not long after, he saw a white curl, a wisp of smoke.

The smell moved along easily on the cold crisp air as he followed the trail of smoke to a cottage chimney. It was a hut really. Thomas saw Helen, too, arriving at the top of the rise and glimpsing the light in the gully below her, just as he did.

Thomas opened his hand and closed it again. Around a branch. He held tight. Gazing down, he saw row upon row of feathers, gleaming white in the moonlight. Now he was right there with Helen. He was an owl holding a bag of coins in his beak. The feathers felt so real that he allowed himself to tip forward, testing. As if in a dream, he plunged downward, falling like a stone until he unfurled his wings and flapped—once, twice, gaining height with every stroke.

Helen wheeled around, startled, but when she saw him it was just as if he'd come into the kitchen before she knew he was home, and she held out her arms to gather him in. Now one of her arms was a perch where he settled, gripping the thick fur of her coat to keep himself steady. Helen took the bag from Thomas and tucked it into her coat pocket.

"I was wondering when you'd get here," she said, rubbing her cheek against his feathers. They watched the cottage in silence, knowing that a hut like this in the middle of the forest was just as likely to house a witch or an evil huntsman as it was a fairy or a kindly old woman. The path the moon cut through the trees ended at a wooden door.

"I have to go in," Helen said. "Don't you agree?"

Thomas was not sure. He opened his mouth to speak, but all that came out was an owl noise—Ooo ooo. He searched his mind for even one fairy tale where the heroine passes a hut ablaze with a fire on a cold winter's night without knocking. He couldn't think of one.

Flapping his wings, Thomas flew to the roof of the hut to indicate his answer. There he sat, on the lip of the chimney, facing outward and away from the smoke, watching Helen approach the door.

She knocked, and Thomas craned his neck to see what would happen next.

"Thomas." Giselle was squeezing his shoulder. "Did you fall asleep?"

Thomas opened his owl eyes and regarded Giselle. Pushing himself up on his elbows, he tried to accustom himself to the light in the room, the warmth of the fire. He concentrated on the creases of skin on her cheeks—Giselle's dimples—trying to remember.

"I know what comes next," he said.

"Will you tell us?" Giselle said, scooting her chair closer.

"Giselle," Mrs. Sharp admonished, "don't crowd him."

Giselle picked up the cold cup of tea beside Thomas and took it into the kitchen. She must have emptied the tea into the sink; when she returned, she made him a fresh cup and placed it on the bricks before going back to her chair. There she sat, bending forward, hands on her knees, waiting.

Giselle could never be an owl, Thomas thought. *She has no patience.*

Turning to face the fire so she couldn't distract him, he told them what had happened.

"You must be a snowy owl," Giselle spoke in a soft voice. "They live in the Arctic."

"I wasn't sure if she should go in, but...I told her to anyway."

"Good work, Thomas," said Mrs. Sharp. "Of course Helen has to go in. She's taking a risk, but certainly whoever lives in that hut knows the woods better than she."

"Thomas, I hate to say it, but I have to go home and practice my cello," Giselle said. "Mrs. Turkalo gets cross when I'm not prepared. Do you know more? Will you save it for next time?"

Mrs. Sharp was gathering up the teacups. "We can work on the story again in a day or two."

Thomas nodded. "She will go in and warm herself by the fire," he said.

It was the least he could do.

Chapter 20

When Thomas arrived home from school the next day, his father was nowhere to be found. He knew his father had been going by himself to the airport when Thomas was at school. He had heard him talking about it to Aunt Sadie on the phone from his spot by the cold air register.

"It's so peaceful there," his father had said. "There's a hill not far from the train trestle with a clear view of the river."

But his father's car was in the driveway.

Thomas called out and there was no answer. He sat in a kitchen chair, wondering what to do as Dave bumped around in his stomach. That's when he noticed that his father's cell phone was on the counter. He picked it up and brought it back over to the table, dialing Aunt Sadie.

"I don't suppose there's any news," Aunt Sadie said by way of a greeting.

"It's Thomas," Thomas said. "I can't find Father."

"Thomas. Duck. Where are you?"

"Sitting in my chair. In the kitchen. He's not here and he's not downstairs. And his car isn't gone." Thomas swallowed, but the swallow didn't go down his throat. It felt like Dave was carrying a big package up the stairs and the swallow met him on the way down and they weren't sure how to pass each other.

"I have an idea," Aunt Sadie said in her in-charge voice. "I want you to check upstairs. In the closet. The one where your mom keeps her winter clothes."

"But..."

"I know it's strange, Thomas, but I found him there once...in that closet. After Helen...left. He goes there to be sad. He's trying to hide it from you...when he's sad. Go and check. Take the phone with you and we'll keep talking."

Thomas tried to take the stairs without his stomach tilting, out of respect for Dave and his package. Aunt Sadie kept talking, telling him that she'd come over after work and that, after they'd located his father, he should take the package marked "Lasagna" out of the freezer.

Thomas pressed his ear to the closet door. He heard something. Even Dave stopped trying to climb the stairs. What Thomas heard sounded like big puffs of air, and in between those puffs, like Mr. Sanders down the street starting up his leaf blower.

Opening the closet door, Thomas surprised his father, who was sitting, holding his mother's maroon blouse, the one she sometimes wore to church in winter. He was using it to wipe his tears.

"Thomas. What?"

Thomas dropped the phone.

His father was crying.

Thomas didn't know his father's eyes had tears. He'd never seen this before. Not when his father fell off the ladder and broke his arm, not when Baby Sadie died. Never. This simple fact caused something to break loose inside Thomas, like an iceberg floating off on its own.

"You don't have to be so sad...it's not over yet..." Thomas struggled to think of something to say, *something* to make his father feel better. "She's not cold either. She has a fur coat."

"What are you talking about?" Mr. Moran wiped his nose with the sleeve of Helen's blouse.

"It was passed down from the first polar bear queen," Thomas said.

"Thomas! You're not making sense."

When his father spoke to him in that tone of voice, it usually made Thomas freeze. But Thomas did not freeze now. He looked at his father's ankles and realized that they were covered in two different-colored socks. They might both look black from a distance, but one was a very dark shade of blue.

Father is crying!

"She's on a quest," he explained, speaking more slowly now. "Mrs. Sharp's helping me make a story about it."

His father stood and dropped the blouse on the closet

floor. Then he stepped out and smoothed the creases of his pants. "Thomas, I repeat. *What* are you talking about?"

The story began to evaporate. Like fog rolling over a field first thing in the morning. Thomas felt his courage, too, seeping away. Dave grew agitated.

His father picked up the phone and glanced at it. "Sadie? Let me call you back." Putting the phone into his pocket, Mr. Moran took Thomas by the wrist and pulled his son behind him. Down the stairs they went and out the front door, leaving it unlocked. Without a coat, Thomas felt the wind sweep up his shirt, but he hardly noticed the cold. There was a storm ahead. He warned Dave to take shelter.

Using his fist, Mr. Moran struck Mrs. Sharp's front door, then stood back. Waiting.

Thomas imagined Mrs. Sharp coming into the alcove and looking through the peephole on her tiptoes.

"Mr. Moran, this is a surprise. Won't you come in?" Her voice trailed away as Thomas's father brushed past her through the alcove and into the foyer.

He stood there with Thomas, his shoulders heaving, trying to pull himself together—to collect himself—as he often told Helen and Thomas to do when they were upset. Cleaning the steam off his glasses with the handkerchief he kept in his pocket, Mr. Moran said in a quiet, controlled voice: "What has been going on over here, Mrs. Sharp? With you. And Thomas."

Mrs. Sharp did not seem to notice his father's agitation.

"It's cold out," she said. "Let me shut the front door. And please, call me Amalia." Turning her back to him, she pressed her small body against the door and Thomas heard the latch click into place.

"Answer my question, please. Amalia."

"Would you like to sit down?" Mrs. Sharp shut the glass door and led them into the living room.

Not waiting for an answer, she continued. "I'll get us some tea."

Sitting on the stool by the fire, Thomas watched Mrs. Sharp's back all the way to the kitchen before turning his attention to his father. His shirt was untucked. And the lock of hair behind his left ear that sometimes stuck straight out before he showered was sticking straight out.

Mrs. Sharp returned, setting down the tray. "Having tea with me is not an indication that you like or approve of what we've done. Nor does it mean this is a social call. But you look as if you could use some, Mr. Moran. Please help yourself. Here you are, Thomas."

"What I need is an explanation," his father began, sitting down in the armchair, but making no effort to serve himself.

Mrs. Sharp took a seat on the sofa and made herself some tea. "Then you shall have one. I was born in Hungary. My parents, both artists, moved to France in 1937 to flee a political regime that was dangerously close to the ideology of the Nazis. But, how do you say this... Out of the frying pan, into the fire. When the Germans occupied Paris and France fell to the Nazis in 1940, my parents were among a handful of Hungarian refugees who joined the French Resistance. They could not stand by, you see, and witness what was being done to our Jewish neighbors without fighting back."

When Mrs. Sharp interrupted her story to take a sip of tea, Thomas glanced over at his father, who seemed to be lulled by her softly accented voice. Mrs. Sharp nodded to Thomas, who understood; he made some lemon balm tea and handed it to his father.

The familiar scent seemed to revive him. "Your point is..."

"My point is...my parents became involved in the resistance effort, smuggling Jews to safety, diverting the attention of the Nazis, until...Well, looking back I suppose it was inevitable that I would become, like Thomas, a child with a parent who had disappeared. After my father was captured, my mother encouraged my brother and me to invent stories about the many ways he could escape from captivity and fight the evil Nazis—she wrote them down for us in a journal—so I can attest to how helpful it can be to find a way to channel—"

"I am sorry for your loss, Mrs....Amalia." Mr. Moran set down his cup. He looked so tired at that moment, as if he might like to lie down on the rug where the couple was taking a walk, even if just for a minute. But instead, he put his hands on his thighs and pushed himself into a standing position. "But you of all people should understand the importance—in a situation like this—of not letting your imagination run away with you."

Mrs. Sharp stood, too. "With all due respect, Mr. Moran.

The imagination will run away with you in such a situation. It is up to us—the adults—to direct it in a positive way."

"I'm afraid on that point we have to disagree. Thomas?"

Though his father reached out his hand, Thomas did not take it. "I have to say good-bye first."

"Fine. I'll wait on the step."

When the front door had closed, Thomas turned to Mrs. Sharp. "He won't let me come anymore."

"No, he won't." Mrs. Sharp put her arms around Thomas. He could feel the bones in her back and for a moment he had the sense memory that he was holding on to his mother. He started to cry.

"You mustn't worry," she said, wiping his tears with a handkerchief she'd produced from her sleeve. "I will be in touch."

"But..." Thomas was having trouble forming words. It felt as though Dave was trying to crawl up his throat again, maybe for a glimpse—just one glimpse—of Mrs. Sharp's living room. "I have to know what happens in the story."

"You have to *decide* what happens. But you must understand, it won't be easy. Like this isn't easy. Your story may be frightening, Thomas. Even dangerous. Every tale worth remembering has hardships, points where...it seems as if... Well, you are preparing for it right now. Helen is about to encounter the first hardship."

"I can't do this on my own," Thomas insisted, holding tight to Mrs. Sharp's sleeve. "You're teaching me."

"Oh, Thomas." Mrs. Sharp pulled him close. "What if I . . . Would you like me to try to imagine what happens inside the hut?" she asked him.

Thomas nodded. "I couldn't find him. And then, he was in the closet . . . My father was crying! That's why I told him about the story."

"You mustn't feel bad about telling him, Thomas. You did the right thing. He loves your mother very much. He misses her. You will hear from me soon. I'll write down what we have so far, and then begin inside the hut . . . If what I say doesn't feel right, you must correct me. It is your story."

Thomas nodded.

"But, Thomas, I'm leaving for vacation this weekend. You see, I always go to my niece's house in North Carolina for the holidays. So that means I—" Mrs. Sharp broke off. "Don't look so sad, Thomas," she said. "For the time being, I will write up what we've created so far, and . . . Let me think about how to get it to you. I'm not leaving for a few days. I'll come up with something."

Later that evening, Thomas pressed his cheek to the cold air register and listened to his father explain to Aunt Sadie what happened.

"I'm still not sure I understand. What was so bad?" Aunt Sadie was saying. "He's a child, Brian. You can't forget that. Maybe he can't take this in . . . logically. He was upset when he saw you in the closet, and I don't think he's accepted—"

"Let's not confuse the issue, Sadie. First of all, I won't be returning to the closet. That is over. What we're talking about here is..."

Mr. Moran fell silent for a moment. His father often told Thomas to consider what he said before speaking. Mr. Moran was considering.

"What is it, really?" he asked. "Magical thinking? From this point on we have to accept what is real. The sooner Thomas grasps what has happened, the sooner we can get beyond it."

Chapter 21

"*Joyeuses fêtes!* Happy holiday break, Thomas!" Giselle called out, running over to Thomas and Martin as they came up Thomas's driveway. "Oh, hello," she said, pumping Martin's hand. "I'm Giselle and you must be Martin. *Joyeuses fêtes* to you, too, Martin."

"And to you," Martin said back. "I think."

"Thomas," Giselle said, holding out a padded envelope, the kind his father's manuscripts were delivered in. "Mrs. Sharp gave me a package to give to you before she leaves tomorrow."

Thomas took the envelope and placed it in his backpack before he opened the side door.

"Can I come in?" Giselle asked Thomas. "I'm starving."

"I think we have cookies," Thomas replied. He had seen his father eating some for breakfast.

"That's odd." Martin stood rooted to the spot outside the side door. "Normally, it's four hundred and twenty-seven steps from your bus stop to your house." Looking over his shoulder, Martin seemed to be retracing the path they'd just walked.

"Four hundred and twenty-seven what?" Giselle asked him.

"Number of steps from the bus," Martin replied. "I'm usually right on the money."

"But you went to knock icicles off the lamppost," Thomas reminded his friend. "Remember?"

"Right." Martin pressed his thumb against the pad of each finger, counting backward. "That's it," he said. "Thank you, Thomas."

"You know how many steps it is from Thomas's bus stop to here?" Giselle was curious.

"As long as Mrs. Pinsky is driving. Substitute drivers can account for a variation."

"Do you count everything?" Giselle asked Martin as they took off their coats and boots on the landing.

Thomas watched Giselle studying his friend.

"Not everything can be counted," Martin replied, hanging up his coat over Thomas's.

Thomas called down the stairs, "We're home. Giselle's here, too."

"Remember to clean up your mess in the kitchen," Mr. Moran called back.

"Where do you go to school, Giselle?" Martin asked as he and Giselle took seats at the kitchen table.

Thomas found a plastic container of molasses cookies and began passing them around.

"I go to the Montessori school," Giselle said. "I might go to the public middle school next year if I can convince my mom it will be okay."

"Why wouldn't it be okay?" Martin wanted to know.

"I had some trouble at my old school. I have trouble with . . . impulse control."

"What does that mean?" Martin asked. "Shouldn't we have plates, Thomas?"

Thomas nodded and got the plates and napkins.

"I bit someone," Giselle said, sweeping the crumbs from the table into her hand and depositing them on the plate Thomas gave her. "But it wasn't impulsive at all. I planned it."

Martin was quiet for a moment. "You don't plan to bite us, do you?" he asked.

"No, silly! Alexis got what she deserved. *Less* than, if you ask me." Giselle had that faraway look that sitting in Helen's chair seemed to inspire before she launched into the story of how Alexis had teased her since fourth grade, pulled her skirt up once in front of the boys, even used some hairs she took from Giselle's hairbrush to make a voodoo doll that she stuck pins in.

"I don't know why she hated me so much," she said. "She just did. And other girls did because she did."

Scooting out of her seat, Giselle extracted the envelope Thomas had hidden away in his backpack and handed it to him. "It's probably because Alexis is mean *and* dumb. She'll regret it later when I am a world-famous psychologist. Then, she'll brag about knowing me. Here, Thomas. You have to open this."

Glancing toward the door that led to the basement, Thomas opened the envelope. Inside was a cloth-bound journal. As he opened the cover a note fluttered to the floor. Thomas picked it up and read:

> *Dear Thomas,*
> *Please study this carefully and you will discover a secret.*
> *I will see you in January.*
> *Sincerely, Mrs. Sharp*

Thomas tucked the note back in the journal. As he flipped through the pages dense with handwriting, Thomas realized he couldn't read the beautifully curved letters—they were written in another language. As he closed the book, the only word from the title he could understand was "Sharp." What had Mrs. Sharp meant? How could he study a book he couldn't read?

"It's in French," Giselle whispered, taking the journal from Thomas and examining the cover. "I take French classes on Saturday, but I don't know this word."

Pulling her phone out of her pocket, she continued, "Just a sec. I need to look something up. Yes, I think in this case *nouvelle* means 'further.' So it's *The Further Adventures of Mr. Sharp*."

"What's the French word for napkin?" Martin asked as he

bit into his cookie. "Because you need one." He pushed a nap-kin across the table.

But Giselle wasn't listening to Martin. She opened the journal to the first page and began to read: "'*Monsieur Sharp était assis sur le train*...Mr. Sharp sat on the train...'" Thomas, do you know what this is?"

"It's the story that Mrs. Sharp and her brother made up about her father after he disappeared during World War II," Thomas said. "Her mother wrote down the story for them. Mrs. Sharp told my father and me about it. But why is it in French? She told us her mother was from Hungary."

"They speak Hungarian in Hungary." Martin regarded his cookie. "These are good, by the way."

"But France was their adopted country." Giselle bent over the pages once again. "Mrs. Sharp told me they never went back to Hungary, so they had to learn how to communicate. Maybe this was a way for them to all practice their French. Mrs. Sharp speaks four languages, you know." Giselle took another bite of cookie. "I would let France adopt *me* in a heartbeat."

"So her father just disappeared? What happened to him?" Martin's gaze traveled from Thomas to Giselle. "Is someone planning to fill me in?"

"No one knows," Thomas said. "He didn't come back."

"Oh." Martin left his seat so he could look at the journal over Giselle's shoulder. "I wonder how she expects you to read it, Thomas."

"I can help," Giselle said.

"But she didn't give it to you, did she?" Martin reminded Giselle. "Mrs. Sharp gave it to Thomas."

"Well, yes, but he can't read French."

"There must be a reason," Martin insisted.

"You're right." Sighing, Giselle pushed the journal across the table to Thomas. "You'll figure out the reason, and when you're done I will translate it for you. My French teacher will help me. Or Mrs. Sharp will."

Thomas took the journal from Giselle and put it back into his backpack. He knew immediately where it belonged: in UnderLand in the metal box with the old coins and the DVD.

That evening, at dinner, Mr. Moran told Thomas he would be getting out the outdoor Christmas lights and checking them. Aunt Sadie was coming over in a couple of days to help put them up. Did Thomas want to help?

Thomas did not. After the dishes were cleared, he excused himself and went to his room.

"I'll be up to say good night," Mr. Moran said.

Lying on his bed, Thomas paged through the story of Mr. Sharp's adventures. The handwriting was even and measured until he reached the middle of the book where the print began to blur. It was as if someone had spilled liquid on the pages.

No. Someone had been crying and their tears had dropped on the ink, causing it to blur. How strange it was that he could not understand a word and yet Thomas knew that the writer was crying.

His father's voice intruded in his thoughts: *You don't have nearly enough information to make such an assumption. They could be drops from a glass of water. Or snow. Or rain. Or even drips from an umbrella. Work from what you know, Thomas. The rest is just conjecture!*

Was it possible to know something without sufficient proof?

Thomas pondered this as his eyes scanned the pages, the letters becoming one long string of shapes. But then he noticed a word written in a different handwriting. It was his name: *Thomas.* He began to scan the unfamiliar words more carefully, running his finger over each line of handwriting. He found another word he recognized, *Look.*

Now his finger moved more rapidly, looking for words that had been written into odd open spaces, like the pieces of a missing puzzle. This must be the way Mrs. Sharp was trying to communicate with him.

He ran his finger along line after line, page after page, and a prickle ran down the back of his neck as he found the words *in her* stuck to the end of a paragraph.

Several pages on, he found teardrops again and the word *favorite* at the end of the page. With only two pages left, Thomas found the last word, *place.*

He closed the journal and opened the blank book Giselle had given him. Carefully, he wrote all the English words in it.

Thomas look in her favorite place.

"Her" had to be his mother. And what was her favorite place? At the kitchen table? Thomas didn't know if the kitchen table was her favorite, but that was surely her place. Without leaving his room, he imagined her chair—but how could he look in a chair? Maybe Mrs. Sharp meant the birdbath? His mother had told Aunt Sadie she sat in that chair so she could see the birds. Could something be in the birdbath right now besides frozen water?

Thomas couldn't risk going into the backyard with his father downstairs stretching lights across the living room floor. If his father discovered what Mrs. Sharp had left for him... Thomas did not know what would happen, but he didn't like to suppose.

Staring up at the ceiling, he felt the fluttering sensation in his stomach and tried to calm Dave by slowing his breath.

"Follow your breath," his mother used to tell him as they lay together on his parents' bed.

"To here," she said, placing her hand on his stomach.

Thomas closed his eyes. That's when he had another strange and magical thought. It was almost as if his mother were in the room, lying next to him.

Once, when they'd been breathing together, he'd opened his eyes and found her watching him. She'd rolled over on her side and propped herself up on her elbow, her face cradled in her hand. Humming softly, she regarded Thomas with a very satisfied look, as if she'd just taken a bite of something delicious.

Thomas tried to remember the words to the song she hummed; it was one she sang to him before he went to bed...

Sleep my child and peace be with you all through the night...

"You're not following your breath," he'd said to her.

"I don't have to, silly. I've found something else to relax me."

"What?"

"You."

Now Thomas did not open his eyes or turn, as he had then, to scoot close to her. It would mean waking up from this moment. He didn't want his eyes to say his mother was not there when something bigger and deeper told him she was.

Chapter 22

Thomas waited for the sliver of light under his father's door to disappear and then gave it an extra ten minutes before he tiptoed down the stairs.

Slipping into his boots and coat, Thomas opened the side door. Outside, his eyes were drawn to the sky. The moon was almost full. It had been snowing earlier, but now the sky was cloudless and the new-fallen snow was bathed in a blue light, with the bare branches of trees etched across the ground, like so many blows of India ink over the watercolor paper they'd experimented with in art class.

Hurrying to the birdbath, Thomas brushed aside the snow to find a plastic bag weighted down by a broken piece of slate. Back inside, safely tucked in UnderLand with his penlight on to see, Thomas unfolded the pages. He skipped over the beginning of the story until he was following his mother down the hill into the gully where the hut sat crookedly, belching smoke.

There was no answer when Helen knocked on the cottage door, so she kept knocking until she finally heard a voice: "If the lady wants to enter, let her enter."

Helen gathered her courage, lifted the latch on the door, and went in. Through a haze of smoke, she saw piles of old shoes, filthy rags, and the form of an old woman standing by the fire.

"I'm searching for the polar bear queen," she said loudly to cover the tremor in her voice. "I'm wondering if you might know the way to her kingdom."

The old woman laughed. "The polar bear queen lives in a land far beyond ours, and travelers must go there without rest. If you so much as fall asleep for a moment, you will find yourself transported back to where you stood the day before. It is an impossible journey, especially for one as delicate as you."

"That may be," said Helen. "But I have to try. I'm hoping she can help me find someone."

"Does this someone have a name?"

"I'm looking for someone named Sadie. And since it is bitter cold out, I wonder may I stop with you for the night?" Helen thought about offering the coins but decided they would be useless out here in the middle of the forest.

So she said, "In return for your kindness, I will give you this." Reaching into her bag, Helen drew out a ball of white wool that gleamed in the weak light of the fire.

"Is it...it is! A skein of wool!" The old woman caressed it with her stiff fingers. She pushed aside her rags until she'd uncovered a basket that held a snow-white sweater. Knit with careful exacting stitches, it was missing a sleeve.

"Now I can finish it!" The old woman was so delighted with her new treasure that she seemed to forget Helen altogether.

"Please, may I stand by the fire until daylight?" Helen asked her.

"Yes, yes. Of course." And through some strange magic, the old crone was able to clear a space in front of the fire and furnish it with a table on which she produced a jug of apple cider and a loaf of bread. When Helen had finished eating, the woman pushed the table aside and produced a clean sheet, which she folded in such a way that it trapped the seeping smoke from the fire. Helen watched it fill until it was nearly the size of the room and looked as soft as a cloud. The woman invited her to lie down on it and rest, but Helen, sensing the old woman was testing her determination, remained standing all night.

As soon as the first rays of sun shone through the panes of the hut, the old woman rose and said to Helen: "Now that you have given me this great gift and have managed to resist sleep though your body longed for it, I have something to aid you on your impossible journey. But first you must eat." She pulled a pot from the coals of the fire, and in it bubbled a rich soup. Helen ate it with what remained of the bread from the evening before, and felt her strength return.

From beneath a pile of worn shoes, the woman produced a pair of clogs. "When you put on these clogs and direct them, they will take you seven thousand leagues in a day. But if you can manage to stay awake for three days, you'll arrive in the polar bear queen's kingdom. When you do, take off the clogs, place them on the ground, and instruct them to return to the woods from which they were carved; instantly they will return home to me and your boots will be returned to you."

Helen put on the clogs, thanked the old woman, and turned to leave, but the old woman was not finished. "Not everything is as it first appears," she said. Placing a fresh loaf of bread into Helen's hands, she continued: "The best thing is not always the best thing. The worst thing is not always the worst thing."

Though this made little sense to Helen, she nodded.

And with that, the old woman closed the door, leaving Helen to resume her journey under the watchful gaze of Thomas, the snowy owl.

Thomas finished reading and thought for a moment before he crawled out from under his bed and went to his desk.

Dear Mrs. Sharp,

Please keep going. Will my mother save the fox on the way to finding the polar bear queen? I think he might be in her story. I hope you have a safe trip.

Sincerely, Thomas

In the morning, Thomas would make an excuse to go to Giselle's house to tell her about the hiding spot and ask her to deliver the letter to Mrs. Sharp before she left for North Carolina.

Chapter 23

Every year that Thomas could remember, Aunt Sadie decorated the outside of the Morans' house with Christmas lights in early December.

"What's the point of decorating an apartment?" she'd say to Helen as she dragged the stepladder out of the garage. "No one can see it."

Thomas and Helen would watch her progress through the living room window. Mr. Moran couldn't look because Aunt Sadie was sloppy about the lights. In a very un–Aunt Sadie–like way, she draped them wherever it was handy—over the drainpipe, on the rim of the roof, down to the yew bushes outside the living room. Every year a different path to lighting up the darkness. She did it like this because that was how their father had done it. And Aunt Sadie wanted to preserve the custom for her and Helen—as well as teach it to Thomas.

"Just think, Brian," Aunt Sadie had told his father. "That's how Santa knows where to bring Thomas's presents. 'Thomas Moran? Oh, that's right. The sloppy house.' "

"No," Helen had corrected her sister. "The house that looks like the night sky. On a clear night. Under a full moon."

The lights were always the same...little white icicles that shone like crystals against the snow.

Now it was Christmas Eve and Mr. Moran had handed them over to Aunt Sadie—tested and untangled. She went outside and stood there looking up, big loops of electrical cord dangling over her arms. The last thing on their mind this year in early December had been decorating the house with lights, but Thomas knew Aunt Sadie believed in traditions. He watched his aunt from his spot by the living room window. She wasn't wearing her Santa hat; she wasn't even wearing gloves.

Finally, he opened the side door for her to come back inside.

"Sorry, Duck," she said. "I thought it would make us feel better, but it just doesn't seem right."

Thomas nodded. He sat down on the landing. Aunt Sadie sat down, too, sliding her back against the door until her bottom was in the puddle her boots made, lights on the floor all around her.

She let her head drop. "I miss my sister," she said. And she began to cry.

From the ache in his stomach, Thomas knew that Dave was crying, too, his head tucked under his wings. Thomas thought about this as he crawled toward his aunt, popping little white lights under the pressure of his knees.

He sat in her lap in the darkness until Thomas's father came up from his office and flipped on the light in the landing. It was so bright, Thomas was blinded for a moment.

No one spoke.

Mr. Moran got a tissue box and the broom from the kitchen. Placing her hands around Thomas's waist, Aunt Sadie moved him off her lap. She went into the kitchen and took her overnight bag and a package of extra lights that hadn't been opened from the table.

"I'll be back," she said, and went upstairs.

But she didn't come back. Not right away. Thomas and his father had their dinner. When they were washing up, Aunt Sadie stood in the doorway.

"I'm going to church . . . to light a candle for my sister."

Thomas and his father hadn't been to church since Helen went away.

On Christmas Eve, they'd always made popcorn and drank mulled cider. They put Duraflame logs in the fireplace and sat with only the Christmas lights and the firelight.

This year, the fireplace was dark. There was no tree. There were no lights.

"Do you . . . want to watch a Christmas special?" his father asked Thomas.

"I'm tired." Thomas was already climbing the steps to his room.

"Here." His father bent to one of the unpacked Christmas boxes, opened it, and handed Thomas a book his mother read to them every year.

"I'll come up in a little while and we'll read."

The book was titled *The Christmas Promise*. He remembered it well. It was about a bad time in history when a man had to leave his daughter behind to search for work. He promised to return by Christmas, and though it looked like he wouldn't keep his promise, he did return. On Christmas Day.

As Thomas walked up the stairs, he realized he did not believe in promises. They weren't observable. Entering his dark room, Thomas climbed onto his bed and set the book on the bedside table. As he lay down, pressing his face into the pillow, something poked his stomach. It wasn't Dave. This was from the outside, a sharpish object, wrapped in a piece of lined paper and tied at either end with a string.

A present?

Thomas sat up and undid the string. The remote control for the outside Christmas lights tumbled into his lap. He pressed the power button; at the edge of his vision, a soft light glowed. He saw that the glow came from beneath his mattress. Like he was floating on a cloud of light.

UnderLand.

Removing the sweater boxes, Thomas scooted underneath. Between the mattress and the metal frame Aunt Sadie had placed the string of white Christmas lights. She must have taken off the mattress and poked each strand through, because the little white icicles dangled above him like caterpillars.

Thomas shimmied over to his usual place. Inside Helen's coat, Aunt Sadie had placed a book, a big blocky book that smelled like old pages.

"Folk and Fairy Tales the World Over," Thomas whispered to himself as he read the title. He opened the book to the first page. On it, his aunt had written:

For Thomas, who will write us a happy ending.

Chapter 24

Four days after Christmas Aunt Sadie came over early and made pancakes for brunch because they were going to launch one last search for Thomas's mother.

"I don't understand why you're going back to the airport," Thomas said into his breakfast plate. "She's not there."

"Don't talk with your mouth full, Thomas," his father said. "I can't understand what you are saying."

Aunt Sadie poured more syrup on Thomas's pancakes. She knew how he liked them. "Brian," she said, "I promised Thomas that he could say hello to Officer Grant when she arrives. It's so nice of her to volunteer to come help us search."

After wiping his mouth with his napkin, Mr. Moran said: "I called and told her to meet us at the airport. It's out of her way to stop here first. We'll drop Thomas off at Martin's as planned and see her there."

"But I thought it would help if Thomas—"

"It's an extra ten miles for her to stop by here. It's her day off, Sadie. We'll tell her you said hello, Thomas."

"You promised." Thomas turned to Aunt Sadie. "You said I could ask her about—" Thomas fell silent. He didn't want to share his thoughts with his father.

"About what?" His father turned to his aunt: "Sadie, what's going on?"

The teakettle that Aunt Sadie had put on began to whistle. She went over to the stove and turned it off. "Remember how Thomas said he didn't think Helen was at the airport anymore? Well, he wants to ask Officer Grant if, when the weather warms up, the dogs will still be able to pick up Helen's smell. That is, is it possible to continue tracking where she went when the snow thaws in the spring?"

"And you're encouraging Thomas to think along those lines?"

Aunt Sadie looked at his father. The expression on her face told Thomas that she was trying to communicate something to his father that she didn't want Thomas to know.

"Thomas. Son." His father reached over and squeezed Thomas's arm. "I don't think—"

"Then let me go to the airport for a minute so I can ask Officer Grant," Thomas interrupted. "It's a good question."

"It's an interesting question and I promise you we will ask Officer Grant when we see her today. Now, please eat your pancakes. You must be hungry. You've hardly touched them."

Thomas pushed his plate away; he was not hungry.

His father pushed the plate back. "It's a long time until supper."

"Maybe some hot chocolate?" Aunt Sadie asked Thomas. She was pouring the hot water into a thermos. "I'm bringing some to the search. But your father bought enough packets for you to have one before we go."

"That's not real hot chocolate," Thomas said. "Giselle melts chocolate bars in milk to make real hot chocolate."

"It says 'hot chocolate' right on the package," his father replied.

Thomas stared at the floor. Why respond to people who didn't listen. About hot chocolate or his mother.

As Thomas got up to clear his plate, he thought he just might be angry enough to drop it on the floor. Turning both spigots at the sink on hard, Thomas watched water splash onto the counter and the floor.

"Thomas! What do you think you're doing?" His father was behind him, turning off the water.

Thomas didn't answer. There was no point. In fact, he wasn't going to talk at all—maybe not until he was all grown and moving out of the house would he speak to his father. And then it would be only to say good-bye.

He would start now and he wouldn't say a word until they found his mother and brought her home. Thomas made a note of the time. Eleven twenty. He would inform Martin of his plan when he was dropped off at his house.

But if I tell him, then I'm talking. No, I can write it in a note.

"What about me?" Dave poked Thomas in the ribs with his proboscis. "You're still talking to me, aren't you?"

You'll be the only one I'll talk to.

Aunt Sadie whispered: "I'm sorry, Duck. I'll make sure we ask Officer Grant."

When Aunt Sadie and his father picked Thomas up at Martin's, he didn't need to ask if they knew more about where Helen was. Nothing had changed.

Thomas put his hand on Aunt Sadie's arm.

"I did ask your question, Thomas," she said. "Officer Grant said it was a good one, too. She made a call to another officer on their K-9 team to get the answer. He told her in his many years of experience he had never seen a dog successfully follow a track that was months or even weeks old. He told her to warn us that people might try to convince us that their dog can—for a price—but not to believe them."

"You mean people actually prey on families that—" Mr. Moran began.

"Yes, that's what she said," Aunt Sadie finished.

At dinner, Thomas pointed to his throat when his father urged him to eat.

Pressing the back of her hand to his forehead, Aunt Sadie asked: "Sore throat?"

Thomas nodded.

"Answer your aunt, Thomas."

"He's flushed. He might have a fever," Aunt Sadie said. "I'll put on the kettle and make him some tea."

"Or he doesn't want to eat his dinner," his father said.

Thomas was saved from further interrogation by a knock on the front door.

"Who could that be? It's Sunday night," his father wondered.

Thomas went to see, opening the front door to Giselle, who exclaimed: "Thomas!" Then, following many French kisses, she whispered: "Il y a plus d'histoire dans le birdbath. Do you understand?"

Thomas did not understand fully, but since birdbath seemed to be the same in both French and English, he guessed that Giselle had received more of the story from Mrs. Sharp and left it for him in the birdbath. So he nodded.

"Thomas? Who is it?" his father yelled from the kitchen.

"Just Giselle!" Giselle called out, putting her mouth against Thomas's shirt to stifle a giggle. "I'll go. My work here is done." She gave him one last hug, then whispered: "But no, it's not! I almost forgot. If you want to write her back, I have Mrs. Sharp's address in North Carolina. Just give the letter to me and I'll take care of it." She winked at Thomas before closing the door.

When Thomas sat back down, a warm mug of tea had replaced his dinner plate. Aunt Sadie's plate was also on the counter. Dave woke with a start as Thomas watched his aunt stir her tea, three times around, then clink, clink, clink; three times in the other direction, then clink, clink, clink. As she laid her spoon in the saucer, just as Helen used to do, pointing in the direction of the birdbath, Dave fluttered to the top of Thomas's stomach and bumped his head.

"How is work?" Thomas's father asked his aunt.

Aunt Sadie shrugged. "What can I say?" She settled her chin in the curl of her palm and stared into her teacup. "It's work."

Mr. Moran turned to Thomas. "I'll put your plate in the fridge in case you get hungry later."

Thomas shook his head. He would not get hungry.

"He's not feeling well," Aunt Sadie said.

"If that's true, then excuse yourself and go lie down."

Thomas mouthed the words "Excuse me," but he didn't say them.

"Thomas—"

"Let him go, Brian. He's got a sore throat. You can take your tea up with you, Duck."

Chapter 25

That evening, after Aunt Sadie left and his father turned off his light, Thomas stole downstairs and retrieved the new pages of his story from under the piece of slate in the birdbath. Back in his room, he wiggled into UnderLand and, with the aid of the Christmas lights, began to read.

The three days that Helen traveled she knew not where were the longest days of her life. As the old woman promised, the clogs carried her swiftly: over mountains, over rivers, over fields. At the end of each day, when the clogs stopped, Helen, overcome with exhaustion, longed to lie down and close her eyes—just for a moment! But she knew if she did, all would be lost and she would not be able to bring Baby Sadie home again. So she propped herself up with the low-hanging branches of trees and let the cold bitter wind sting her cheeks as she ate a few bites of bread from the loaf the old woman had given her.

Thomas followed her, winging his way over the trees. On the third evening, Helen found herself in a clearing at the edge of a dark forest. The old woman had told her she'd be in the polar bear queen's kingdom after three days. Setting down the clogs, she bid them return to the woods from which they were carved and watched them fly off. As they were soaring through the air, Helen's boots dropped from the sky. She plucked them out of the powdery snow and pulled them on. When the first light of dawn broke, Helen set off through the forest again, keeping the sun to her right cheek and wondering how she would find the queen.

The snow was deep and Helen was so very tired it was an effort to hold up her head. From far above in the treetops, Thomas thought she looked like an old woman.

If her head hadn't been bent so, Helen might have missed the drop of color, like a half-buried feather from a cardinal's breast. Immediately she knew it was blood.

Helen stopped, holding her breath. Waiting.

In the silence and stillness of new-fallen snow, she thought she heard something. Was it? Yes. Like a cat licking its fur. She followed the faint noise until—not far away— below a tangle of brush she spied a young fox licking at his bloodied paw, which as she drew nearer she could see was caught in a trap.

Helen fell to her knees and crawled toward the fox, who, mistaking her for a beast in her great coat, raised the fur on his back and bared his teeth at her.

"No," Helen whispered. "Hush."

Confused by her scent, the fox stopped growling and simply waited for what would come next—the final blow? The gunshot? Helen's fingers crept out from the sleeves of her coat and took hold of the rusted spring on the trap, working to release the animal. The fox cried out as the trap sprung free. Hurling the trap away in case the hunter should come back for it, Helen sat there on her knees wondering what she could do for the little fox. His paw was still bleeding.

"I have to leave you," she said finally. "You must stay still and rest and keep that paw in the snow until the bleeding stops." Helen broke some of the bread into small pieces, which the fox licked off the snow.

"Stay here and heal," she said. "When I have found Sadie, I will come back."

Stroking the fox's head, she looked into his eyes.

What pain she saw there!

"I will come back," she repeated. "I would never abandon an injured comrade."

Thomas folded the sheets of paper and put them into his metal box, considering. He didn't like the word "comrade." His mother never used that word. He would say something to

Mrs. Sharp about changing that sentence. What should it say? Maybe: *You will never be in pain again.* No. How could he say that? There was no way to predict what the fox might have to suffer.

Thomas let his mind drift. He was following an old scent. There was no smell, but still...He thought about his aunt and how she'd cried on Christmas Eve. At dinner, in addition to the way she stirred her tea, he'd noticed there was something wrong with her hair. It was always pulled back into a pony-tail, neat and shining, but now it looked dull and there were white flakes in it, like his father sometimes got in his hair. There had also been a smear of oil on her blouse. His aunt, who never wore anything unless it came out of a dry cleaner bag, was wearing a dirty blouse.

He went to his desk and tore a sheet of paper from his school notebook.

> Dear Mrs. Sharp,
> I think Giselle was right after all. It isn't Baby Sadie that Helen needs to save. It is my aunt Sadie. There's something wrong with her. It's like...she has the clouds in her eyes.
> Sincerely,
> Thomas
> P.S. Please change the word "comrade" to "friend."

Chapter 26

January was cold and snowy; and yet butterflies appeared to Thomas everywhere. He cut butterflies out of salted butter and ramen noodle wrappers. Catalogs, gift bags, sympathy cards, old cooking magazines—they all begged Thomas to transform them into butterflies and save them from being dumped into the noisy recycling truck that lumbered down their street every other Thursday.

Thomas granted their wishes, smuggling the paper and cardboard into UnderLand, snipping wings after his father's light went out and piercing the little cardboard bodies with Helen's bobby pins. Giselle was his inspiration—her skirt, her jacket, her sunny moods, even her anger. Whenever he'd tried to draw her as a butterfly, Thomas felt limited by his drawing skills and the flatness of the surface. She had so many moods that butterflies and the extra clippings that were not butterflies piled up around him.

Thomas decided to take a butterfly with him on the first day back to school. This particular butterfly had been born from a midnight-blue greeting card and the writing—Thinking of you—was in gold glitter. Thomas had torn off the front and used his thumbnail to press a fold into the cardboard. He'd cut carefully so that as much of the glitter as possible would stay on the butterfly's wings.

It comforted Thomas to slip the butterfly into the front pocket of his backpack; he knew that his father was meeting before school that morning with Mrs. Evans, Principal Bowen, and the school psychologist, Mr. Feeney, in the office to discuss Thomas's refusal to talk.

Though he sat in the reception area waiting, Thomas could hear snippets of their conversation, such as "normal reaction" and "monitor the situation." Mrs. Evans told Thomas as they walked to class that she would find a way to accommodate him. "For the time being, Thomas," she said. Thomas knew she would make it her personal goal to be the one to "fix" him.

After the bell had rung and students got out their journals, Thomas thought about giving the butterfly to Mrs. Evans so that she would go easy on him. He reached into his desk and ran his finger over the smooth and rough surface of the wings.

"Answer the question on the board in your journals," Mrs. Evans told the students after the morning announcements, leaning back in her chair and pointing in the direction of her whiteboard.

As he sat at his desk—not writing—Thomas watched George tap Bella on the shoulder and ask to borrow a pencil when he clearly had pencils of his own. It was widely known that George liked Bella—was that why he teased her so much? Thomas didn't know what Bella thought of George, but judging from her expression when she turned around, he guessed not that much.

Thomas pulled his butterfly out of his desk. Using the eraser end of his pencil, he touched George's shoulder.

George turned around. "What?"

Handing George the butterfly, Thomas gestured toward Bella. He showed George that it was a bobby pin.

George took the butterfly in his hand. After considering for a moment, George tapped Bella on the shoulder again and offered it to her on his outstretched palm. She took it and looked at him, confused. Then she turned back around. Neither Thomas nor George knew what would happen next.

"And why is Bella's journal of such great interest, Mary?" Setting down her book on designing backyard playgrounds, Mrs. Evans huffed her way to standing.

"It's not, Mrs. Evans. I'm sorry," answered Mary, turning back to her work.

But something that could distract Mary Mallender from her full-time job of being perfect was something that intrigued Mrs. Evans. So she made her way over to Bella's desk.

As it turned out, it wasn't Bella's journal that was attracting attention; it was her pencil. Mrs. Evans held out her hand.

Bella had wound one of those small rubber bands girls put at the end of their braids onto her pencil and slipped the butterfly bobby pin into it.

"Very interesting." Upon examining the pencil, Mrs. Evans looked down the row to Thomas. Only she knew who supplied a steady stream of butterfly questions to the Ask Mrs. Evans box.

"Thomas." Mrs. Evans took a step closer to his desk. "Do you know anything about this?"

Thomas looked up at Mrs. Evans. He did not like to lie. Or, in this case, tell the truth. So he did what he was good at. He waited.

"I see." Mrs. Evans thrummed her fingers on his desk, trying to figure out a way to get Thomas to talk.

"You've got the wrong kid," George informed Mrs. Evans. "I made that. For Bella. Is that a crime?"

"In my classroom, Mr. Panagopoulos, distraction is a crime, but it was nice of you to do this. Much better than scaring her with a tarantula." Mrs. Evans returned Bella's pencil and asked her to put the butterfly away.

"Did you know," she continued, looking directly at Thomas, "that some people call a group of butterflies a kaleidoscope and others call it a swarm or a rabble? Such colorful words. Which do you prefer, Thomas?"

The class waited for Thomas to answer. Except for Martin, they didn't know yet about his not talking. He was hoping to keep it a secret for a while since he was very quiet anyway as a rule.

"He likes rabble," George said, coming to Thomas's aid once again. "Don't you, Thomas?"

Thomas nodded his head. He knew, of course, what a group of butterflies was called, and he definitely preferred "kaleidoscope." But he also preferred being helped rather than having his shirt grabbed, so he gave George a thumbs-up.

Later that evening, safely tucked away in UnderLand, Thomas pondered the events of the day. Did his butterfly change the story of Bella and George? Reaching to his side for a butterfly, he used the bobby pin to clip it to the bedframe. Then he fit another next to it, so that the wings overlapped slightly. Then another and another until all the butterflies he'd made so far clung to the mesh above his head, interspersed with the icicle lights Aunt Sadie had put there at Christmastime.

"Do you think my mother will like this?" Thomas asked Dave. "It's a kaleidoscope."

"I do," Dave replied. "Very much."

Chapter 27

The next day after school, Thomas sat at the kitchen table watching his aunt drink tea again. She had picked Thomas up from school, but instead of running errands and going to the gym, she just brought him home and made herself a cup of tea—Fog Mountain tea, by the smell of it.

Thomas put his hand on his aunt's arm. She didn't look up. She didn't put her hand over his and say, "It's okay, Duck." She just kept looking into her tea. Dave was playing some sort of game with a piece of toast Thomas had just eaten, tossing it up, catching it, tossing it again.

It was the first time Thomas wished he hadn't stopped talking. But what would he say if he hadn't? "It's okay," when it wasn't? Or "It's going to be okay," when he had no proof that it would?

"What is Giselle doing in our backyard?" Thomas's father had pulled back the curtains and was staring out the window.

Going over to stand by his father, Thomas saw Giselle in her purple jacket lying on her back near the birdbath. She was kicking out her legs and swishing her arms back and forth over the snow that fell last night.

Dave forgot about the toast; his antennae tickled the sides of Thomas's stomach, as if he were trying to get a glimpse of Giselle, too.

"Thomas?" His father held out a pad and the pencil he'd tied to a string and taped to the binding.

"Snow angels," Thomas wrote. "Can I go out, too?"

"And why, I wonder, is our yard better for snow angels than hers?" his father replied, which meant yes, Thomas could go.

Since Thomas had stopped talking, his father said yes to most things. This was not normal for them. His father also didn't remind Thomas to put on his snow pants or to put his wet clothes in the dryer after.

He just sighed, poured another cup of coffee, and headed down the basement stairs, leaving Aunt Sadie to clink the spoon against her teacup alone.

Thomas noticed that he was rushing to get into his snow clothes. Slamming the side door, he ran out to the backyard.

"I was hoping you'd see me and come outside," Giselle said. "Mrs. Sharp got back this afternoon and asked me to deliver a package for you."

Thomas looked into the birdbath and saw the pages

enclosed in plastic. Glancing toward the house, he decided it wasn't safe to retrieve them just yet.

Giselle lay still, her eyes closed, as if she were asleep and having a lovely dream. It started to snow again and Thomas watched the snowflakes settle and melt on her flushed face.

She had ringed the birdbath with angels, their wings touching, forming a chain like the ones they made out of construction paper in church. Thomas fit himself into the angel next to Giselle and stretched out his arms until his fingers grazed her sleeve.

"Thomas, I'm making you a work of art. Do you like it?"

Thomas nodded.

Giselle sat up and studied him, her hair covered in lacy flakes. "Still not talking?" she said. "Look up, Thomas. Look at the snowflakes. See how they fall together like they're kissing?"

Thomas watched the flakes as they floated down in no particular hurry. The sky was cloudy and the silver, patterned flakes appeared suddenly, like dancers from behind a gray curtain. Every once in a while they collided and joined, producing two tiny wings. Thomas sat up.

Pressing on the surface of the snow to pack it down, Thomas took off one of his mittens and, with his finger, wrote: *I want to make a butterfly that can go outside in winter.*

Giselle lowered her head to see what he'd written. "Hmmm...a butterfly who can go outside in winter. Maybe with snowflakes for wings?"

He nodded again and put his mitten back on.

Giselle was quiet, studying him. "My mom and I have a crafting table," she said finally. "We could try to make one."

Thomas nodded. Running back to his house, he went into the kitchen with his boots still on.

"Thomas?" his father called up. Aunt Sadie did not lift her head.

He wrote "At Giselle's" on the pad, tore the paper off, and let it flutter down the basement stairs. Then he ran out the door again, leaving his wet boot prints on the kitchen floor.

Chapter 28

By the time Thomas got home from Giselle's, Aunt Sadie was gone. His father made dinner, and after they ate and did the dishes, he returned to his office to finish his work.

Thomas snuck outside to get the plastic bag containing the next installment of his story. He took it to his room, moved aside the storage boxes, and crawled into UnderLand. Turning on the Christmas lights, he began to read.

After Helen said good-bye to the fox she got to her feet. Standing next to her was a massive polar bear, far larger than the one who'd met her at her car.

"Are you—" Helen began.

"Yes, the one you've been seeking. Do not be afraid, my dear; I will not hurt you," said the polar bear queen. "It was your kind act toward this little fox that summoned me. Come close and let me warm you." Helen let herself be

wrapped in the bear's embrace. "You've come such a long way. And yet...and yet...I have to tell you, Helen, your baby is not in my kingdom."

Helen pressed her face to the polar bear's sleek fur and began to cry.

"Go ahead and cry. What else can we do when nothing is as we imagined it would be? But you did not come this long, difficult way in vain, Helen. Your quest is just different than you thought. Are you afraid of what lies ahead?" The queen turned her head so that she could regard Helen with one great brown eye.

"A little," Helen said. "Will it hurt?"

"I'm afraid so, but change is often painful, isn't it?"

Helen nodded. She didn't like change.

"In order for you to go home, you must save three lives. Unbeknownst to you, you have already begun by springing the trap for this fox."

Helen nodded. She'd come this far. She must continue to be brave. With a glance up at Thomas, who was watching and listening from a nearby branch, she took a step back and straightened her shoulders, waiting for what would come next.

"Then...you wish to go on?"

Helen nodded. "I do."

"You must find the other two that need saving." And with that, the polar bear queen disappeared into the snowy landscape.

Helen beckoned to Thomas. "Where will I find them?" she asked when he'd landed on her shoulder.

More than anything, Thomas wanted to help his mother, but he did not know, any more than she did, which way to go. Once again, Helen said good-bye to the fox, and with Thomas still on her shoulder she walked through the snow until they came to a rutted lane worn from the tracks of sleds passing through.

They followed it, and before long they heard a commotion coming from beyond a hedge of dead wood and brambles. As they came closer, they saw a farmer cursing his pony. Harnessed to a plow, the pony strained mightily but couldn't make a dent in the frozen furrow. The man showered the pony with blows until she buckled and collapsed on the ground. Helen started plunging into the snowdrift, parting the brambles with her bare hands, calling out to the farmer to stop. Thomas flew to a branch of a nearby tree.

"What business is this of yours?" the farmer asked, waving the stick at Helen.

Thomas was about to dive at the horrible man, to let him feel his sharp talons, but then he realized this pony might be one of the lives Helen had to save before she could return home. So he waited nearby, ready to defend his mother if it was necessary.

"Have compassion, sir. This pony is too weak to do as you ask."

"Not after a taste of this stick."

"No." Helen grabbed hold of the man's arm. "Let me buy her then."

From inside her coat pocket, Helen produced the bag of coins that Thomas had provided. She handed it to the farmer, who took the bag and pulled out a coin. "What's this, then?" He held the coin close to his face. "You're not from around here. What use have I with these? They'd laugh in the marketplace if I tried to use them. Keep your coins." He tossed the coin and the bag at Helen, who watched as they sank into the snow.

Helen knelt down by the pony. She stroked her knotted mane. "There must be something I have that you want. Would you...would you accept my coat in exchange for your pony?"

No! Thomas did not like this idea. He winged his way to the space between them and settled on the ground. Helen mustn't give this awful man her coat.

"Such a coat could warm me through the deepest cold," he said, eyeing it appreciatively. "But she is a fine pony. Add the owl to the bargain and you'll have a deal."

"The owl is not mine to give. It will have to be the coat or nothing." Helen stood and began to remove her coat as if the deal were sealed. And it was. The man threw down his patched coat and held out his hand for Helen's. After handing hers over, she picked up his old coat and put it on.

Delighted with his deal, the farmer strutted up and down the row. But Thomas could only think of Helen, her small figure inside the thin coat she now wore. How would it keep her warm enough?

"It's time for my lunch. You'd best be gone when I come back."

Thomas watched the man walk away as Helen knelt in the snow urging the pony to stand. She broke up the last of her bread and offered it up on the palm of her hand. "You must be starving, poor thing."

Licking at her hand, the pony opened her eyes. She tried to lift her head.

"We'll stay here until you have regained your strength." Helen tore a piece of cloth from the hem of her dress. Dipping it in snow, she began to wipe the blood from the pony's flank. "You will get through this. You will," she murmured. "We're here now. I'm going to call you Sadie after my sister. She's the strong one, isn't that right, Thomas?"

Helen unbuckled the harness and they waited for Sadie to revive. By and by, she did and, after several tries, rolled herself up to standing. With slow careful steps, Helen led the pony to the road, and they were on their way once again.

As Thomas flew overhead, scanning the ground for what danger might come next, he watched as Helen and the lame pony struggled in the deep snow. Neither figure seemed to have the strength to carry on. But when he flew closer, he could see they were leaning into each other for *support and warmth, just as Helen had always done with her sister.*

Thomas wriggled out of UnderLand, folded the papers, and stuck them in his back pocket. He needed to get a message to Mrs. Sharp right away. They must find a way to help his mother.

Thomas retrieved Giselle's coins from the box, went downstairs, and put his coat on before he found his father in his office. Tearing a page from the pad on his father's desk, he wrote: "I have to return these to Giselle. She let me borrow them."

Taking the bag of coins, his father said, "For a school project?"

"No," Thomas wrote. He paused. He hadn't realized that all this writing gave his father evidence of anything he might say that wasn't exactly true. "I like to look at old things."

"You do?"

Thomas nodded.

"And it has to be tonight? It's eight thirty."

Thomas nodded.

"Go on then, but come right back." His father looked as if he'd like to say more, but he stayed silent.

Once outside, Thomas ran until he reached Giselle's door.

Nadine answered his knock, holding a jar that smelled like rotten eggs. "Hello, Thomas. I'm having some kimchi. Would you like some?"

Thomas shook his head.

"You should eat something fermented every day. It's good for your gut."

"Who is it, Mom?" Giselle appeared at her mother's side. "You're not eating that awful stuff in front of Thomas." Pushing the jar away, Giselle crinkled her nose. "It's so stinky."

"I'm sorry optimum health offends you, my dear." Ms. Dover kissed the top of Giselle's head.

"Come on." Giselle led Thomas into the kitchen, where a much nicer smell was coming from the stove.

Handing Giselle the bag of coins and the folded sheets of paper, Thomas sat down on a stool and waited for Giselle to read what Mrs. Sharp had written.

"Oh no. She'll freeze to death for sure."

Thomas pulled out a small pad and pencil he'd begun carrying around in his back pocket and wrote: "I wanted her to find Aunt Sadie, but she found a pony instead. Why didn't the coins work? And why did she have to give up her coat?"

"Maybe a snack will help you think your way out of this," Giselle suggested. "I made apple cider and spiced it with cloves and cinnamon sticks."

She reached for the cupboard door, but Thomas held her arm and pointed back to his paper. "What if my mother blows the whistle?" he wrote. "Do you think this means it's the right time?"

Giselle poured their cider, thinking. "I don't know."

"The bear said she could only use it once," Thomas wrote on his pad.

"If the bear doesn't come to help, do you think your mom and the pony can stay warm enough? I hate to think what will happen to them when night falls."

Thomas knew that the bear would save his mother if she blew the whistle. Why then did his mouth suddenly go dry—as if the powdery scales Dave shed from his wings had settled on his tongue—when he thought about it?

He took a deep breath and wrote:

Dear Mrs. Sharp,
Do you think it is time for my mother to blow the whistle?
Sincerely, Thomas

Chapter 29

It was more than five weeks since Helen disappeared and eleven days since Thomas stopped talking. Aunt Sadie was driving Thomas to school; she'd spent the night the evening before because it had been Helen's birthday and none of them had wanted to be alone.

Turning into the school parking lot, Sadie grazed the cement curb, trying to get as close to the sidewalk as possible. Before Thomas could get out of the car, he saw Principal Bowen hurrying toward them, waving. It made Thomas feel queasy the way she walked, like she had bad news to convey.

Dave flopped to the bottom of Thomas's stomach and said, "What could be worse than Helen?"

True.

Aunt Sadie lowered her window, and Principal Bowen leaned in. "Sadie, I'm so glad I saw you out the window. You saved me a call to Thomas's father. I wanted to let him know that Mrs. Evans has taken her maternity leave early and the long-term sub starts today. He'll be with us until the end of the year. Since you're here I thought perhaps you'd like to meet him. He's in my office now. Will you come in for a minute?"

Aunt Sadie glanced at the digital clock. "Sure," she said. "But I'm short on time." Pulling into a parking spot, she turned to Thomas. "I'll come in and decide if he gets the Torini stamp of approval." Thomas's backpack bounced on her car horn as she tugged it off his lap. "Remember, Thomas," Aunt Sadie continued as they walked into the school, "no matter what he says, you don't have to talk. You have the right to remain silent."

There weren't enough chairs in the principal's office for four people to sit down, so Principal Bowen excused herself to get one from the teachers' lounge.

After she left, Thomas and Aunt Sadie stood facing the young man who would be Thomas's new teacher; no one was sure what to do without Principal Bowen to oversee the proceedings.

"I'm Jason," the man finally said. "Jason Walters." Thomas worked his way up to Mr. Walters's face as his new teacher shook hands with Aunt Sadie. "I'm cool with Jason, but they have a formality thing at this school, so we'll stick to Mr. Walters for now."

Mr. Walters had shiny blond hair and blue eyes and a sunburn. His nose was peeling, Thomas observed.

"You don't look old enough to be a teacher," Aunt Sadie said.

"I'm not, actually. I'm fifteen. But, Thomas, please don't tell Principal Bowen."

Mr. Walters made Aunt Sadie laugh.

He winked at Thomas. "I know my secrets will be safe with you."

"Here we are." Principal Bowen came back into the room, chair first. "I've told Mr. Walters about your...silence, Thomas, and he's fine with having you continue to write your answers instead of speaking them aloud. That is...until..."

"We understand." Aunt Sadie gave Thomas his backpack and they both sat down. "Sorry, but I'm on the clock here."

"That explains it." Mr. Walters turned his blue eyes on Aunt Sadie.

"Explains what?"

"Why your hands are so warm. You're a shallow breather."

Principal Bowen slid into the chair behind her desk. "If we could return to the subject of Thomas's silence, Mr. Walters."

"If you don't mind, Principal Bowen, I'd like to hear this."

After receiving a "This better be good" look from Principal Bowen, Mr. Walters took the seat next to Aunt Sadie. "People who are 'on the clock,' as you say, are often in a state of chronic stress. It's low-level, but your body can't differentiate. Under stress, blood flow is redirected from the heart to the limbs so they can take action."

"And what does a long-term sub who just graduated from high school know about chronic stress?"

"Not much," Mr. Walters replied. "I studied medicine for a while before I decided to chuck it all and travel."

"All I ask is that you . . . take care of my Thomas."

Mr. Walters nodded. "You have my word."

As Thomas was pondering what it meant to *have* another person's word, Principal Bowen gathered a few sheets of paper on her desk and stapled them. "Yes, well," she said, which meant they were at the end of their conference.

"About this grief you feel, Thomas, I—"

"Thank you, Mr. Walters." Principal Bowen stapled her sheets of paper a few more times. Turning to Aunt Sadie, she said: "Thanks for taking the time to meet with us, Sadie."

After Mr. Walters left for the classroom, Aunt Sadie stood outside the principal's office buttoning her coat. "At least he's not a know-it-all, like Mrs. Evans," she said. "No . . ." Rummaging through her purse for her keys, she continued: "He's of a higher order than that. I have to stay late at work today, Duck, but I'm coming over again for dinner." Kissing the air near the top of Thomas's head, she turned and left the building.

When Thomas entered the classroom, he noticed that Mrs. Evans's piggy bank for UNICEF, her footstool, and her jumbo carton of hand-sanitizing wipes were all gone from the room. Mr. Walters didn't seem to have brought anything, not even a coffee cup.

As Mr. Walters wrote his name on the board, Thomas noticed

that he wore a plaid shirt under his sweater; his belt should have kept his jeans at the right height, but still they seemed loose.

Turning around, Mr. Walters sat on his desk and pulled his legs up cross-legged. "I don't like to sit in chairs as a rule," he said.

"Then why do we have to?" George asked.

"Evolution before revolution..." Mr. Walters examined the name card on George's desk. "George. Let's learn my rules first, shall we? One: Don't use a simple word when a more complex one will do. If you succeed at this, we can do away with vocabulary tests. Two: When I ask a question, you get extra credit if you also write down your answer. If you succeed at this, you'll get plenty of writing practice and we won't need our daily journal. Three: I've decided to relocate the United Nations to this classroom, so we don't have to bother with geography. Be thinking about which country you would like to represent as ambassador. Four: Our official world sport is soccer. Known to the rest of world as football..." Mr. Walters paused to consider the bewildered faces of the class.

"Are you storing all this in your gray matter?"

George did not bother to raise his hand. "In the U.S. of A., Mr. Walters, the official sport is football. The *real* football."

"Is that so?"

"I vote for basketball," Weston Behling suggested. Weston's father had gone to college on a basketball scholarship. It was one of Mr. Behling's favorite topics during social hour after church.

"My mother says it will always be baseball, first and foremost," Mary Mallender added. "Shouldn't we be raising our hands, Mr. Walters? Or are you an anarchist as well as a soccer fan?"

"Very good, Mary. Get out your devices to look up 'anarchist' if you don't know what it means. No, I'm not. In this class, I'm the president of the United States, and I just signed this into law." Mr. Walters held up a piece of paper that looked suspiciously like the daily lunch count. "This is an executive order declaring soccer the official sport of the United States."

"You can't do that," George said.

"Yes I can. Or, wait a minute. No, I can't. When you tell me under what conditions the president can bypass Congress and sign a bill into law, we'll be on our way to dispensing with government lessons."

At this point, several students spoke at once.

"I hope you haven't figured out how to get rid of math," Martin said. "It's the only subject I really like."

"Excellent. You can help me convince the haters, um... Martin."

The students fired off several more questions.

"How old are you?"

"Irrelevant."

"Why are you sunburned?"

"It's summer in South America."

"Can you sign an executive order to make recess longer?"

"You tell me."

"Are you a hippie?"

"Yes and no. Depending on the definition."

"Are you gay?"

"What makes you think that?"

"Well, you have long hair like a girl's and you wear necklaces."

"Also irrelevant. However..." Mr. Walters reached into his shirt, pulling up the medallions that hung around his neck. "Would you like to see my necklaces? We'll need a quorum for me to put them on display. I got them in Bolivia."

No one knew what a quorum was, but the vote was unanimous.

Chapter 30

As he rode the bus home after school, thoughts of Mr. Walters and the way he taught fifth grade filled Thomas's head. He was so familiar with the path from the bus to his driveway he might have stayed distracted until he'd reached the side door.

But today, without even looking closely, he knew something about the view of his house had changed. A tall rectangular box sat propped against the front door. Glancing over at Mrs. Sharp's house, Thomas wondered if she'd left something on the stoop. No. She would know it was impossible for him to sneak a package like that into the house.

Thomas approached the box. It looked like a proper package, with a mailing label and a bar code on the side. Oh. The package had his name on it. He took a few steps back.

Thomas thought for a moment. It was better for his father

to discover it when he brought in the recycling bin from the curb that night when Aunt Sadie was there.

For the briefest of moments, Thomas allowed himself to hope.

Could this be a good thing?

He didn't indulge in that feeling for long, but forced himself to think about his chores, the weather, Mr. Walters's strange homework assignment.

"I'd like to get to know you as quickly as possible," Mr. Walters had said, passing out strips of poster board eleven inches long and three inches wide.

"Print your name on this card and bring it in tomorrow along with three things you love. I'll take a photo of each one of you surrounded by your special things and *voilà*, you're completely unique—not just a name."

"What if the thing we love is big—like my dirt bike?" George wanted to know.

Mary Mallender raised her hand. "I have a Great Dane," she said, "but they only allow special-assistance dogs in school."

"If it's too big or it's not allowed, bring a photo of it."

As Thomas took off his coat and hung it up, he thought about what he loved. His mother, his father, Aunt Sadie, Mrs. Sharp, Giselle, Martin; but they were people, not things.

This box on the front porch then? Thomas felt as if he loved the box without even knowing what was in it.

"What is going on?" Dave unfolded his wings and flicked them against the sides of Thomas's stomach—like butterfly kisses. "Are we inside? Have you made an X on the calendar yet?"

After dinner, Aunt Sadie was doing the thing with her tea again. Stir, stir, stir. Clink, clink, clink. Breathing through his mouth so he didn't have to smell dirty socks, Thomas watched his father watch her, watched him listen to the stirring and the clinking and decide whether to say anything.

"I'm going to get the recycling bin," Mr. Moran said finally, and left the room, returning a moment later, kicking at the door with his foot.

There wasn't space on the counter for the box, so Thomas cleared his plate and pushed Aunt Sadie's to the side. When his father set the box on the table, Thomas could no longer see his aunt.

"I didn't order anything," Thomas's father said. "Sadie, did you have anything sent here?"

"No," came the answer from behind the box.

Squinting at the small print on the label, Thomas's father said: "All it says is that it's from ADV Processing. But it's got our name on it. In fact, it says 'Attention Thomas Moran.' Thomas?"

Thomas shook his head.

"Hand me that knife on the counter."

Even though his aunt was closer, Thomas moved around her to reach the knife.

After his father sliced through the tape, both he and Thomas leaned in to get a look at the contents. But all they saw was another box top, this one shiny white.

"Keep hold," his father instructed as he reached into the box, and Thomas held the sides so his father could pull out a white box revealing the glossy photo of the Revolutionnaire Classic Food Processor on its side.

Placing the larger box on the floor, Thomas's father said: "Can someone enlighten me?"

Thomas shook his head and stared at his fingers on the placemat waiting to see what would happen next. It absolutely positively *was* something good.

"I can't think who—" his father began.

"Of course not. You'd have to use your imagination."

"For God's sake, Sadie. Snap out of it. Even if it were meant for Thomas, what would he do with it? We hardly need a food processor for the two of us."

Rubbing her temples, Aunt Sadie said, "Return it, then."

Thomas stared at his father. The presence of the machine— the *actual* machine and not the image of it on the DVD—had the strangest effect on him, as if Dave was down in his stomach blowing bubbles. It tickled him inside, and the ticklish feeling curled up the back of his neck.

"Thomas! Why are you smiling? What is going on here?" his father said.

Dave stopped blowing and rolled over onto his stomach, curling his wings over his body.

"Thomas, I'm not angry at you. I'm just trying to—"

His father was waving the notepad Thomas used to answer questions. "Who did you tell about the DVD you and your mother watched?"

Thomas turned around and reached out his hand for the pad. He picked up a pencil and wrote: "It's mine. It has my name on it. I want Aunt Sadie to take it to her house and teach me how to use it."

His father took the piece of paper, read it, and handed it to his aunt. "That's not a viable plan, Thomas. Your aunt doesn't know how to cook any more than I do."

Aunt Sadie kept her head down. She flipped over the piece of paper, grabbed the pen, and printed in large capital letters. "Aunt Sadie will learn."

She put her arms around the box and stood up.

Thomas ran to the pantry and grabbed his apron, the one his mother had sewn for him, from the hook below where his mother's apron hung. He always wore that apron when he and his mother cooked together. Returning to Aunt Sadie, he set the apron on the box.

"I'll pick him up Saturday afternoon for our first lesson."

Chapter 31

The next morning, Thomas sat on his bed, wondering if he'd chosen the right things to help Mr. Walters get to know him. If he was making an oral presentation in front of the class, Thomas would bring the magic set Aunt Sadie had given him for Christmas the year before last. It had trick dice and a box that made dollar bills disappear. He'd bring the Detroit Tigers pennant his father put up on his wall, and maybe the framed photo of him and his mother and father with their faces poking through a triceratops, T. rex, and mastodon cut-outs at Dinosaur World.

But since it was just Mr. Walters and he *did* say he wanted to get to know him, Thomas had chosen *The Big Book of Laughter and Happy Things* from Giselle, a picture of a Karner blue butterfly he'd torn from the pages of an old *National Geographic* magazine, and a photo of him and his mother in the backyard.

The photo was taken during a year they weren't sad. His father had bought a new camera that spring and snapped picture after picture for no good reason: Helen watering the hydrangeas, directing the hose spray in the air so that Thomas could dance beneath it; Thomas and Helen in a staring contest; the two of them on their backs blowing bubbles; even one of his mother and father holding hands on the front step that Mr. Moran had asked Thomas to take.

Thomas slipped the photo with the bubbles and the picture of the little blue butterfly into Giselle's book and was about to put it all in his backpack when he remembered the DVD of Chef Philippe in the metal box. For some reason, he tucked that in, too, found space for the notebook in his backpack, and headed off for school.

As Thomas made his way toward the front entrance, he saw Mrs. Templeton drop off Martin, who rushed to join him, clacking and jangling. Thomas pointed to his abacus under one arm and his game of Chinese checkers under the other. Then he held up three fingers so Martin could supply the third thing he loved.

"What else?" Martin asked him. "My M&M bag collection. I've got a photo of it in my backpack."

Martin loved to count the colors in a party-size bag of M&M's. If a kid happened to bring a bag of M&M's for dessert at lunchtime, Martin could estimate, with reasonable accuracy depending on the processing facility, how many of his or her favorite color they could expect to eat.

During sustained silent reading, Mr. Walters took his phone out of his pocket and called Bella Atkins's name.

"Bring your three favorite things with you into the hall so I can take a snapshot," he told her, grabbing a stack of papers from his desk and following her out the door.

Thomas tried to concentrate on his book about code-cracking during World War II, but his mind kept wandering back to his story. Through Giselle, Mrs. Sharp had relayed to Thomas that she would wait until he decided about the whistle before writing more. It was his story. Thomas found himself wishing there were clear-cut rules for how to proceed, like the ones his father used when he was copyediting.

As the morning wore on, Thomas noticed he wasn't the only one who wanted to keep his favorite things a secret. Gary exited the classroom with a long vacuum cleaner box that surely did not contain a vacuum cleaner; Mary Mallender had something big and heavy in a pillowcase.

They all returned smiling, as if they'd just been told a good joke or were remembering something funny from a movie they'd seen last night. When it was Thomas's turn, he grabbed his backpack from underneath his chair and went into the hall.

"So what have you brought, Thomas?" Mr. Walters was sitting at the student desk Mrs. Evans kept in the hall.

Thomas reached into his backpack and handed Mr. Walters *The Big Book of Laughter and Happy Things*.

"Someone made this for you." Mr. Walters turned the pages slowly until Thomas and his mother and the little blue butterfly fluttered out.

Retrieving the pictures, Thomas handed them to Mr. Walters, who kept on flipping the pages even though there was nothing in the book but the one line from Mrs. Sharp's story. When he turned his attention to the pictures, he said: "This must be your mom. She looks like your aunt. And this...You like butterflies, do you?"

Thomas nodded.

"Excellent. So you have this book, the photo with your mom, and your favorite kind of butterfly?"

Thomas held up his finger. Leaning in, he turned to the back of the book until he came across the DVD. Thomas pulled it out.

"I see." Mr. Walters accepted this bonus favorite thing. "'Meet your new Revolutionnaire,'" he read aloud. "'The at-home advanced food processing system, with all new recipes by famed chef Philippe Duprée.'" He looked up at Thomas: "So, you like to cook, too?"

Thomas reached into his back pocket for his notebook. "My mother and I used to watch this," he wrote.

"Hmmm." Mr. Walters finished reading Thomas's note. "So it's a favorite thing because it reminds you of your mother...Well, it's an obvious choice, then. So, how will we pose you, I wonder. How about...you here..." Mr. Walters pressed Thomas back against the wall. He handed the book to Thomas to hold.

From the student desk Mr. Walters pulled out a package of the sticky stuff they used to put up posters.

"Your name here." He tacked the strip of poster board just

above Thomas's head. He stuck the picture of the butterfly and the DVD in big gold stars that he fixed to the wall over Thomas's right shoulder. "Okay, this looks good."

Backing away, he held up his camera, framing the shot. "Excellent. Now, let's put this photo of you and your mom right by your shoulder. Better yet, lower, right by your heart."

Mr. Walters backed away again. "Whenever you're ready."

Thomas waited for Mr. Walters to tell him to smile, but that instruction didn't come. So he nodded and Mr. Walters took the photo.

"Perfect." He showed it to Thomas, who observed that he did not look happy with his beloved things.

So why is it perfect?

Carefully, Mr. Walters removed the DVD from the gold star and put it back inside Thomas's book.

"I used to be a cook," he said. "A line cook on a cruise ship. You know how much people eat on a cruise? We had a dozen food processors. There was no way we could have kept up with the demand otherwise."

Tucking the photograph and the picture of the Karner blue between the pages, he said, "Thank you for sharing these things with me." Then he handed Thomas the book and the homework assignment he'd completed the day before.

How long had they been out there—just the two of them in the hall? Thomas went back to class feeling the way he imagined the other students had.

Not happy, maybe, but good.

Thomas took his seat and picked up his library book. He was trying to find his place when George passed by his desk and knocked his writing sample to the floor attempting to balance a football on his index finger. The assignment had been to write about a moment that held personal meaning. Thomas had written about the day their soccer team won their first and only game. Martin scored a goal with assistance from Thomas. The Templetons and the Morans celebrated with ice cream sundaes.

As he picked it up, Thomas saw the comment Mr. Walters had written on the back of his paper: *You must know that what happened to your mom is not your fault. Do you know that, Thomas? In your heart?*

Chapter 32

Once, when the Morans' car had broken down on the way to Grandpa Moran's funeral, Thomas and his mother and father stayed in a hotel. It was the kind of hotel business people stayed in when they had to be out of town for weeks at a time. It had a kitchenette with dishes that couldn't break and a couch that pulled out to make a bed. There was a vase with flowers made out of fabric and trapped in gooey stuff that looked like water.

Aunt Sadie's apartment reminded Thomas of that hotel. Everything in its place. She was a lot like his father in that way.

On Saturday, Thomas was in the kitchenette in his stocking feet, staring at the Revolutionnaire box along with Aunt Sadie.

"I guess we should start with the instruction manual." Aunt Sadie cut the tape, opened the box flaps, lifted out the Styrofoam, and pulled out the lid, which had a feed tube.

She handed it to Thomas; as he turned it over, a part fell off. *Did I break it already?*

"Don't worry." Aunt Sadie studied the illustration from the instruction manual. "I think it's supposed to come apart. Hey, here's a DVD. Want to visit your old friend Philippe?"

Aunt Sadie seemed relieved to move away from the machine and over to the couch opposite her big-screen TV.

Thomas wondered what Philippe would look like on such a big TV. He'd only ever seen him on the little one that his mother and father had in their bedroom.

But in place of Philippe, a woman dressed in a T-shirt and a sunflower apron appeared on the screen. She had long blond hair in a ponytail tied in such a way that it spilled over her shoulder. Her name was Ashley Prentiss. The announcer said she was a raw food chef from Atlanta, Georgia, and creator of the blog Flashley.com, where thousands of people visited every day to heal themselves of everything from migraines to acid reflux.

"There is a living spirit in the food that we can harness to heal us," Ashley said. In a soft Southern drawl, she told the listeners of her own digestive problems, which began in childhood with strange pains in her stomach every time she ate, and then she moved on to how to make crackers out of sprouted grains.

"She's the upgrade? Seriously?" Aunt Sadie grabbed the remote. "Can you believe this, Thomas? I'd much rather learn to make artery-clogging French food.

"Where's the menu?" Searching until she found "Using

Your Revolutionnaire," she and Thomas watched Ashley demonstrate the same basic procedures Philippe had: how to lock the work bowl and lid into place and hold the blades by their hubs.

They watched in silence, letting Ashley fill up the empty air with her exclamations: "You can't mess this up. " "Here's a trick I learned from my time at the ashram."

Next to him, Aunt Sadie began making a funny huffing noise as her shoulders moved back and forth. Thomas put his hand on his aunt's arm.

"I know your not talking has something to do with your...sadness about your mom," she said between sobs, because she was truly crying now, tears running down her face and her nose running, too. "But I can't take it, Thomas. I really can't. You're the only one I have to talk to. When Helen stopped...well, when she basically stopped talking, it was just you and me. And now...I feel like I've lost both of you."

Hiding her face in her hands, she continued: "I'm sorry. I just had to say that. It's okay. We're both sad. We're just sad... in different ways." She looked up at Thomas. "We'll make it through this."

Looking at his aunt's red-splotched face gave Thomas a feeling like Dave was rolling his wings around himself like a blanket. Flopping onto the floor of his stomach, Dave's muffled voice reached Thomas.

"Do something!" his butterfly pleaded.

"I have an idea," Thomas whispered.

Aunt Sadie tilted her head and regarded Thomas: "Go." Sniffling, she pointed the remote at the screen and pushed the off button.

"Maybe I can only talk when I'm with you . . . Maybe . . . it's magic."

"I'll take it." Tossing the remote onto the couch instead of putting it in the basket, Aunt Sadie moved over to her kitchen table. Thomas put the loop of his apron over his head. It wasn't long enough anymore—the ties hit him at his ribs—but he didn't mind.

"Now let's figure out how to work this baby." Adopting Ashley's Southern drawl, Aunt Sadie continued: "Place the work bowl on the base—off center."

"She said *left* of center."

"Right. I mean left." Wiping away the last of her tears with the sleeve of her blouse, Aunt Sadie put the work bowl on the base and clicked it into place. "That was satisfying. What happens next?"

"'The lid of your food processor has a feed tube that the food pusher fits into.'" Thomas read aloud from the instruction manual as he held up the parts for Aunt Sadie.

"Highly technical, but I think I understand."

Running his finger along the side of the work bowl, Thomas said: "Note the interlock mechanism. You have to put the lid just to the right of the mechanism. Now turn it counterclockwise and it should click into place."

Aunt Sadie did as she was told. "I like the way it clicks.

It's like instant feedback. Didn't we watch a show once where they taught cats how to do tricks using a clicker?"

"With my mo—" Thomas said.

Just like that, Thomas was transported to the Morans' worn comforter, the flickering light of their television at the foot of the bed, and his mother nestled between him and Aunt Sadie.

He stood there, frozen. The knowledge that this experience, which seemed like such an ordinary occurrence to be enjoyed on any evening, was gone from him—maybe forever—took his breath away.

Grabbing Thomas, Aunt Sadie wrapped him in a hug. "It's okay. That happens to me, too; it feels like, all of a sudden, you're standing at the opening of a big dark hole."

Aunt Sadie did not let go of Thomas. "It's okay," she said again. "Breathe, Thomas."

Thomas could not say how long they held each other and did what people do every day without even thinking—breathe in, breathe out—and he waited for Dave to stop fluttering his wings at the bottom of his air pipe. Aunt Sadie took Thomas's face in her hands and asked, "Okay to let go?"

Thomas nodded and she picked up the food pusher, stuck it into the feed tube, and pressed the on button. "Why won't it turn on?"

Thomas swallowed. "You have to push it down hard to make sure it is engaged."

"I did that. So why won't this stupid thing turn on?"

"You have to plug it in, too."

"Duh." Aunt Sadie reached across Thomas to grab the cord and plug it into an outlet.

Thomas and his aunt practiced using the pulse button.

"Shouldn't we cook something with it?" Thomas asked.

"I guess so."

They moved to the refrigerator, which was filled mostly with white light, but also a plastic bowl with some cut-up fruit, a container of yogurt, and a couple of takeout boxes from General Tso's Chinese Palace.

"Well," Aunt Sadie said. "We can't make zucchini noodle spaghetti or raw falafel or any of the other disgusting things that Ashley makes. Let's see..." Yanking open the vegetable crisper drawer at the bottom, she pointed to a bag. "I have some baby carrots. We can practice with those."

So they inserted the shredder disk and Aunt Sadie loaded the feed tube with baby carrots. Handing Thomas the food pusher, she said: "Have at it."

Aunt Sadie pushed the button as Thomas pressed down hard. In less than a minute all of the baby carrots had become shreds of carrot. There was a moment of silence as they stared into the work bowl.

Now what? Thomas wondered. Aunt Sadie's lower lip was nipped under her teeth.

"By the way," he began. "I have a butterfly in my stomach. His name is Dave."

Pushing back his bangs, Aunt Sadie asked: "Why does he stay down there in the dark?"

"Because it's safe."

"I see. I don't suppose butterflies like shredded carrots."

Thomas shook his head. "Or frozen casseroles," he said. "Or Texas toast."

"I wonder if Dave likes minestrone soup," Aunt Sadie mused. "You know, the kind they have at Tuscan Express? With the buttered breadsticks?"

Thomas nodded. He thought so.

"Let me get my dry cleaning together and we'll go get some. That's enough practice for one day, don't you think?" Disappearing into her bedroom, Aunt Sadie returned moments later with her arms full of blouses and pants, frowning. "But . . . does the magic work in restaurants, too? Will you be able to talk in Tuscan Express?"

Thomas sat down on the couch, pressing his hands to his knees and his face to the back of his hands until it hurt, waiting for the right answer to come.

Yes, the magic said to him. *I work at Tuscan Express.*

"I think," Thomas said, lifting his head, "the magic is you."

Chapter 33

The following Tuesday, Mr. Walters approached Thomas after the final bell rang. "Heading for the bus? I'll walk you."

Thomas shook his head as he pulled his coat out of his cubby. It was Aunt Sadie's day to pick him up.

"Did you leave this on my desk when we had recess?" Mr. Walters asked, holding out an envelope.

Thomas nodded, keeping his eyes on the note.

"Do you want me to read it now?"

Thomas nodded again, waiting as Mr. Walters slid his finger under the envelope flap and tore it open.

" 'Dear Mr. Walters, will you teach me and my aunt to make something in our food processor? We don't know how to use it.'

"Hmmm . . ."

George jogged past them.

"Your idea for turning our math homework into a fantasy

football league has promise," Mr. Walters called after George. "I like your initiative."

Without turning around, George saluted his teacher.

"What does your aunt say about this?" Mr. Walters asked Thomas.

Taking his note back, Thomas grabbed a pen from his backpack. "You are the only person we know who can use one," he wrote. "Plus, she says you're of a higher order." He didn't add "than Mrs. Evans," which is what Aunt Sadie had really said.

"You haven't told her about this plan, have you?" Mr. Walters waited for Thomas to shake his head.

"There you are, Thomas." Aunt Sadie came into the classroom, shifting her purse so she could put her arm around Thomas.

"Hello, Jason."

Mr. Walters tucked Thomas's note into his pocket. "Hello, I was just...Thomas wrote something about a new food processor."

"Oh, right. We have to go by the store, Thomas. Have you decided what you want to make?"

"So you're going right now...to the store?"

Aunt Sadie nodded. "Yes. The store. Where they have food."

"The food store. Nice. It just so happens that I am a whiz at food processors since I used to work on a cruise ship."

"You were a chef? On a cruise ship?"

"A line cook would be more accurate. But I do know my

way around an S blade, and Thomas asked if I would help teach you. I'm happy to offer my services." Mr. Walters put his hands in his pockets and smiled at Aunt Sadie.

"Thank you, but I'm sure we can muddle through on our own."

Thomas tugged on Aunt Sadie's sleeve.

"Can't we, Thomas?"

Thomas shook his head, got out his pad, and wrote, "Please."

"Depending on where you live, I could be at your place at four thirty or so...after the staff meeting and one quick trip to a friend's?"

"Well..." Thomas could see his aunt was flustered. She hadn't planned on this. "What would we make?"

"May I humbly suggest a strawberry tart with lemon curd and a pecan crust?"

"Lemon what? Do they have that at Thrifty Acres?"

"They have the ingredients. Tell you what, I'll give you a quick list since I know you're going to the store and I'll put your address into my phone. Go."

Mr. Walters pulled out his phone and stood at the ready.

Aunt Sadie set down her purse and drew the lapels of her coat together. "Really," she said. "You don't have anything better to do?"

"It's either cook with you or go home and hang out with my mom, who's been watching the soap *Metro Medical* since she was a teenager."

"Hang out with your mom," Aunt Sadie repeated. "Fine. Give me the list."

Aunt Sadie pulled out her phone and Mr. Walters dictated to her. "I'm trusting you already have things like sugar," he said. "But since you might be one of those frightful margarine people, let's add real butter. Nothing in a tub—the stick variety. Oh, and unsalted, please."

Aunt Sadie added "butter" to her list. "What about strawberries?"

"That's why I have to stop at my friend's. He grows them."

"No one has strawberries yet," Aunt Sadie said with great authority.

"What can I say?" Mr. Walters winked at Thomas. "It's magic."

Aunt Sadie looked at Thomas. "Speaking of magic, does the magic still work if we have a guest, Thomas?"

Something bubbled in Thomas's stomach. As if Dave had been drinking fizzy water and burped.

"Thomas? Was that a giggle?" Aunt Sadie asked. "Well, we won't keep you. 723 N. Fox Avenue, Apartment 2B. That will be four thirty?"

"Or so," Mr. Walters said.

"Or so" turned out to be 5:18. Aunt Sadie wasn't pleased. She consulted her watch. "I'll have to call your father," she said before opening the door.

"*Voilà.*" Mr. Walters handed Aunt Sadie a shoebox filled with strawberries.

"Um, could you take off your shoes?"

"With pleasure. My socks, too?"

"That won't be necessary."

"It'll be great to air my feet." Mr. Walters said this from his position on the ground. "I prefer being barefoot." He'd slipped off his shoes and was now sitting cross-legged on Aunt Sadie's doorstep, pulling off his socks.

Aunt Sadie tried to close the door. "If you could just move in a . . ." But Mr. Walters's attention was on his feet, which he was now massaging.

"Shoes are terrible for your feet," he said. Then, seeing the expression on Aunt Sadie's face, Mr. Walters asked: "What? Am I breaking a rule? Why are you looking at me like that? Is it my toes?" He stuck his legs out straight to give them a better view. "It's true, my second toe is longer than my first toe. It's a condition called Morton's toe. Did you know that since ancient times those with a longer first metatarsal were considered more clever and creative than other people?"

Aunt Sadie shook her head. "I had no idea. Did you, Thomas?"

Thomas shook his head as well. "I've never seen a teacher's toes before."

Mr. Walters jumped to his feet. "Thomas, did you speak? Can you say that again? I want to hear the sound of your voice."

"I said, 'I've never seen a teacher's toes before.'"

"This is great! Should we sing something? I want to hear your singing voice."

Aunt Sadie went into the kitchenette. Thomas heard water running, then her voice: "It's not permanent. Explain to Jason, Thomas."

"It's magic," Thomas told his teacher. "I only talk when I'm with Aunt Sadie."

Thomas expected more questions, but instead Mr. Walters said: "Then it's even more important to sing to keep your voice in shape. What should we sing?" Mr. Walters started to hum. "How about a camp song? What camp songs do you know?"

Thomas shrugged. Aunt Sadie leaned over the counter. "Thomas never went to camp. By the time he was old enough, it made Helen anxious to—" She broke off.

"Then I'll teach you one. Let's see. How about 'She'll Be Comin' Round the Mountain.'" Mr. Walters started to sing, slapping his knee and singing about driving six white horses and wearing red pajamas and calling out "yeeeee-haw." Thomas sat on the couch, listening.

So this is what you do at summer camp?

"Oh my God. Jason, where did you get these strawberries?" Aunt Sadie held a green stem in her hand; the other hand was under her mouth to catch any possible drips.

"I told you, it's magic," he said, taking a rubber band from around his wrist and putting his hair into a ponytail. "Time to cook?"

Thomas followed Mr. Walters into the kitchen, where Aunt Sadie had put the strawberries into a colander. "I feel like they'll melt in my mouth."

"That's because you're used to supermarket strawberries that have been bred to travel thousands of miles. My buddy grows the old-fashioned kind in his solar greenhouse. You can't stack these in a truck."

"But I can eat them. Try one, Thomas."

"Go ahead, Thomas." Mr. Walters put his face in the colander and took a big sniff. "So where is this grand food processor you're so excited about?"

Aunt Sadie pointed at a cupboard. "In the appliance garage," she said.

"Appliance garage? Nice. There's a first-world phrase for you." Mr. Walters found the Revolutionnaire. "I love these things," he said, running his hands over the sides of the work bowl. "Did you get the ingredients?"

Aunt Sadie took the ingredients out of her shopping bag and set them on the counter. "These look rotten," she said, pointing to the package of dates.

"They may look rotten, Sadie, but appearances can be deceiving. Dates are delicious."

"I'm not the world's most adventurous eater," she warned him. "Can we please get on with this? Thomas is going to be late for dinner."

Mr. Walters hopped up to sit on the counter. "We could eat the tart for dinner."

"I don't think so, and as a teacher, you must appreciate having a schedule."

"As a teacher, I appreciate not scheduling things when I don't have to."

"His father will be waiting."

Mr. Walters saluted Aunt Sadie and hopped down from the counter. "Let's have a look at these dates. Nice. They leave the pits in to keep them fresh longer." Washing his hands, Mr. Walters explained: "You can open the flesh with your fingernail and then pinch."

Taking turns at the sink, Thomas and his aunt washed their hands.

"We'll need a cup of them," Mr. Walters instructed.

When they were done he dumped the dates into the food processor and told Aunt Sadie to press the pulse button five times.

She kept her finger on the button until Mr. Walters said, "Let's review the definition of the word 'pulse,' Sadie."

"I am not one of your students, Jason."

"I hate to say this, but with regard to cooking, you might be. Plus, what's wrong with being a kid? Am I right, Thomas? I liked being eleven."

"He's not eleven yet." Aunt Sadie pressed the pulse button again. "You can probably remember that age quite well."

"You're really hung up on my age, aren't you?"

"I'm not hung up." Aunt Sadie finished pulsing. "There. It looks like goo."

"Not done yet. Thomas, your turn." As Mr. Walters measured out the pecans and put them in the work bowl, Thomas changed places with Aunt Sadie.

"Now, show us what a pulse is, Thomas."

Thomas tried to pulse the way Philippe did, pushing the button down quickly several times, like Dave opening and closing his wings when he was happy.

"Excellent. Ten more times. I'm twenty-seven and you're, what, thirty . . . ?"

"Thirty-four. I don't even know why we're talking about this."

"That's perfect, Thomas! They're ground up together. Do you have a little oatmeal, Sadie? It's just a bit moist."

"I've got one of those instant packets."

Mr. Walters sighed. "My work here is cut out for me, Thomas."

It took two hours to make the strawberry tart. Aunt Sadie had to call Thomas's father twice to say they were delayed. Thomas had never seen so many dishes. The crust was pressed into the bottom of a pie plate, then they made the curd, which sounded awful but looked like lemon pudding. Cutting up the rest of the strawberries, Mr. Walters tossed them with sugar until they glistened. Then he poured the fruit over the curd.

They didn't eat it, though. It had to chill. All that work and Mr. Walters didn't get a bite.

"It doesn't matter," Mr. Walters said when Aunt Sadie told him it wasn't fair. "I licked the spoons when your back was turned. Of course, we could make it again. If you're a hands-on learner, as I expect, you'll only master it after you've made it on your own. With my encouragement, of course."

"I think one strawberry tart is enough."

"I think it's a good idea," Thomas said. "Maybe you could teach us pizza crust, too."

Chapter 34

After school the next day, Thomas and Martin were finishing up a card game of war in his kitchen when Giselle knocked on the front door and opened it before Thomas had a chance to do it for her.

"Thomas..." She paused, out of breath from running. "I asked Mrs. Sharp again about the whistle for you—how you would know if it was time—and she said—" Giselle broke off when Thomas put his finger to his lips.

Giselle clapped her hand over her mouth. "Your dad," she whispered. "Sorry."

Thomas shook his head.

"Your aunt?" It was a good guess, but wrong again. Giselle moved Thomas aside and walked to the kitchen. "Martin!"

"Hi, Giselle. Do you want to play war with us? The more players the better."

"On any other day that would top my list, Martin; but

today I just need to speak to Thomas—privately—for a minute." She stepped back into the hallway, closing the door to the kitchen, and lowered her voice again to a whisper. "She wrote down some questions for you."

Thomas unfolded the sheet of paper Giselle had extracted from her coat pocket and began to read: "Things to consider: What magic does the bear possess that might help Helen? Do you know how he will help her out of this predicament—?"

Martin opened the door. "What are you guys doing? Don't you want to—what is that, Thomas?" He pointed to the piece of paper in Thomas's hand.

As Thomas handed over the piece of paper to Martin, Giselle said, "Thomas, are you sure you want to do this?"

Thomas nodded and proceeded into the kitchen while Martin read.

When he was done, Thomas took the paper in Martin's hand and wrote on the back: "It's time to tell Martin about the story. I need more help. If I get the story now, will you read it aloud?" He handed the paper to Giselle to read.

"Sure," she said, after she'd finished. "If that's what you want…"

Thomas nodded and went to get the story from the metal box beneath his bed. As he brought it to the table, he could see that Giselle had found a bakery bag of sugar cookies on top of the fridge. She removed six and put them on a plate, which she set in the middle of the table, next to the stack of playing cards.

Martin was silent as Giselle read aloud. More silence followed after she'd slid the pages across the table to Thomas.

"I vote to have her blow the whistle." Giselle spoke first.

"Me, too," Martin agreed. "Blow it yesterday."

"But what will the bear do when he gets there?" Giselle asked, licking sugar from her fingers.

"He gave Thomas's mom the coat, didn't he?" Martin reasoned. "He's bound to come up with something."

"I agree. The bear will do whatever it takes."

"You have to be quiet while I think," Thomas wrote, before crossing his arms on the table and putting his head down.

Go there!

Thomas assumed the rustling noises around him meant that Giselle and Martin were getting comfortable. He didn't care. His eyes were closed and his nose was touching the surface of the table.

They're on the rutted road...

Thomas listened to the hum of the refrigerator. His mother and the pony had been walking when he'd left them, leaning against each other. His mother was shivering. The pony was huffing big hot breaths of air, trying to warm her.

This is where I come in.
The owl circled up high at first, then descended slowly.

He could see that Helen was shivering, one hand interlaced in the pony's mane.

She held out her arm for Thomas to land, but instead he flapped his wings to distract her and managed to get the bag from her neck. He lifted the bottom of the bag and watched the whistle tumble out. Clutching it between his talons he showed it to Helen, trying to get across that she needed to blow it now.

Helen grabbed for the string, but missed. "There are so many things you don't understand," she said. "It isn't time yet! Don't do it, Thomas!"

But Thomas had stopped listening—all he could see was how cold his mother was. He placed the whistle on the ground and blew and blew. It was so much harder with a beak!

A shadow loomed over Thomas. The polar bear had come.

"Oh, Thomas," Helen cried, her teeth chattering. "What have you done?"

After one long, sad look at Helen, the bear's sharp claw made a cut down the middle of his chest—so deep that the bear now stepped out of his coat altogether, revealing his dry black skin.

Unrecognizable from the great majestic beast he had been only a moment before, the polar bear now looked like some prehistoric monster.

"Thomas, what have you done?" his mother said again, and sank to the ground, burying her head in the fur.

The bear was disappearing now, into the woods, leaving his coat behind for Helen to use to protect herself from the cold.

"No, no, no." She stood, gathering the coat to her. "He has given me everything and kept nothing for himself."

Thomas sat up straight and blinked. He looked at Giselle and Martin looking at him. Why? Why of all possible outcomes was this the one that came to him?

I don't want this story!

"I shouldn't have blown the whistle," he wrote, and underlined it. "Now the polar bear will freeze to death."

Dave agreed with Thomas, fluttering his wings and looking for an opening so he could leave Thomas alone with his poor choice.

"He doesn't *have* to die, does he?" Martin asked. "Mrs. Sharp hasn't even written it down yet. You can just change it or find a way to make him safe."

Thomas put his head on the table. He didn't think he could just erase what he'd imagined in the story. He heard Mrs. Sharp's words: *"Every tale worth remembering has hardships, points where . . . it seems as if . . . Well, you are preparing for it right now."*

But what was he preparing for? He didn't know and he didn't want to know. He clutched his stomach. He just didn't want to make another mistake in the story.

Giselle grabbed Thomas by the hand. "You have to go see

Mrs. Sharp," she said. "You *have* to talk to her so she can help you find a way to fix your story. We'll write a note for your father that we're going over to my house. I can read jokes to Martin and . . . we'll call his mom so she picks him up from there. That will give you plenty of time."

Thomas nodded. He wrote the note for his father and set it on the counter, willing Dave to be still. He *had* to concentrate. Somewhere in the astral plane an innocent bear, a lame pony, and his mother were in danger. And it was all because of him.

Chapter 35

As Thomas approached Mrs. Sharp's house, he heard her voice coming from the backyard. It sounded like she was calling out to someone. He waded through the snow to peek between the slats of the tall wooden fence. A whirl of color and motion appeared before him as birds lifted and settled like sheets drying on the line. There were feeders on poles, feeders hanging from trees, whirligigs twirling furiously. Bright spots of color—red, blue—darted from tree to bush to fence perch. In the middle of all the bustle and activity stood Mrs. Sharp, her figure outlined by the gray siding on her house, calling out to the birds to come closer. She opened her coat and pulled a handful of seeds out of the pocket of her apron, offering it up to the sky.

A small bird landed on the tips of her gloved fingers before dropping down into her palm to take the seeds. It was so small Mrs. Sharp could close her hand and conceal it like a magician, making it disappear. But she didn't, and soon the tiny bird hopped up her arm to the crook of her elbow, as if making room for more at the table.

Thomas stood completely still, mesmerized by the birds. He allowed himself a few minutes to take it all in before he opened the gate, sending the birds into a frenzy of flight, scattering seeds everywhere. Mrs. Sharp came over and shut the gate, pulling Thomas into her yard and the shelter of her embrace.

"Thomas, dear." Hugging him tight, Mrs. Sharp said, "This is what I wanted to hire you for," she whispered. "Do you think you would like this kind of work?"

He nodded into the folds of her coat.

Mrs. Sharp took his hand and led him into the house. "Giselle told me you'd stopped talking. I wonder if you could make an exception for me?"

Dave's antennae tickled the top of his stomach. "The answer is 'yes,'" he told Thomas.

"Yes," Thomas whispered, following Mrs. Sharp into her kitchen.

"Very good." She turned and smiled at him before placing the teakettle on the stove. "Let's hang up our coats and you should take off your shoes and socks, Thomas. I'll give you a nice warm pair of socks to wear while we dry them."

Once they were settled in the living room, Mrs. Sharp asked Thomas to tell her what was wrong, and it spilled out of him: how desperately upset Helen was with him; the naked bear, who was sure to die of cold now that he no longer had fur, and how *he*, Thomas, was the cause of it all and didn't know how to make it right.

"Do you think it's been you all along who has caused this unhappiness?"

Thomas couldn't answer. There was that feeling in his throat again. Like Dave and the big package...on the stair. He hid his face and began to cry. A torrent of tears came out of Thomas. It came from a place deep inside him. Dave bumped around, collecting them in buckets.

When the storm subsided a little, Thomas told Mrs. Sharp about the times when he'd gotten angry at Helen for forgetting to bring the snack to soccer practice; or when he'd thrown a tantrum to get her to look at him. To *do* something. He told Mrs. Sharp every bad black thing he could think of and how afraid he was that he would never be able to apologize to his mother for the hurtful things he'd done.

And when he was done he lay down and rubbed his teary face on the rug. And waited.

Finally, Mrs. Sharp spoke. "My father had a very particular step. One of his feet was not formed properly and it dragged just a bit. He could hide it, but he never tried in the hall outside our apartment because he was coming home to his family.

"After he disappeared, we'd often hear his step only to discover it was the milkman or the landlord, but not our father. As the days stretched into weeks and then months, a strange thing happened. Instead of thinking about when he'd return,

I began to remember...the times I'd withheld my good-night kiss. Or when I refused the doll that he'd paid too much for because she had brown hair like mine and not blond. I couldn't go back and change these things. It caused me such pain.

"That's why my brother Josef and I told stories about my father's adventures.

"Creating a life for him was how we kept my father with us. Someday Giselle will translate the stories in the journal and you'll see. It's all there."

"I didn't want Helen to freeze to death, so I blew the whistle even when she begged me not to. Now the bear will freeze."

"I see your predicament," Mrs. Sharp said, rubbing his back. "But it is a story, Thomas. You can re-direct it just like you changed Helen's quest for Baby Sadie to Aunt Sadie."

"But I don't know how—none of the pieces fit together yet."

"May I suggest that while things may look very bleak at the moment you will, with time, find the right ending."

Thomas couldn't look up at Mrs. Sharp. He concentrated on the flames. "My mother is dead, isn't she?"

"I believe she is." Mrs. Sharp sighed. "She was sick for a long time. You do understand that what she had...was not something she could help, Thomas. Or you or your father or your aunt could prevent."

Thomas was quiet for some time.

"She doesn't die in my story," he said.

"I think your story has become real for you. That's what

we ask of good stories, isn't it? That they become real to us and that we live inside them for a time?"

"But how can they be saved?"

"I don't know. Whenever we reached the edge of the cliff, as my mother would say, we took a break from the story and made an apple strudel. We made a dough that stretched so thin you could see your hand through it. All the kneading it took! Using your hands is good for solving problems. I know you're unhappy now with the choice you made about the whistle, but put your story out of your mind again and an answer will come to you...seemingly out of the blue."

Thomas took the tissues Mrs. Sharp handed to him and began to wipe his face.

"Others will have their opinions, Thomas. But in the end this is your story, just as this is your life. Helen didn't choose to be depressed. And there are things that you didn't choose, too. However, this story belongs to you and you are the author. When you understand that completely, you will have a power that is, well...it is something like magic. Now let's get our coats."

After they were bundled up, Thomas followed Mrs. Sharp into the kitchen were she got some gloves and an apron. "Here," she said, tying the apron on over his coat. "Why don't you try feeding the birds since you're here? It can be our secret. First, we'll just stand quietly while we wait for them to get used to you. That will give me time to tell you a story. Put on the gloves and you can borrow my boots. I have another pair.

"It's a war story," Mrs. Sharp continued once they were

outside, "but I didn't hear it until after the war. It's about my mother's niece, Nora, whose family moved from Hungary to Holland before the war began. I guess resistance runs in our family, because Nora joined the Dutch freedom fighters at only nineteen years old. She was arrested and put in prison in 1940. Her parents were expected to do her laundry, so they came to get her dirty clothing once a week, riding thirty miles each way on a bicycle with wooden wheels.

"Nora was so clever! She figured out how to send notes to her family by inserting tiny letters inside her clothing labels. I have one; would you like to see it?"

Thomas nodded.

Disappearing into the house, Mrs. Sharp returned with a scrap of paper pinched between her fingers. "You'll need this to keep it from blowing away." She placed the tiny note in Thomas's palm and put a magnifying glass over it.

Moving the glass, Thomas watched the foreign words swim across his hand as Mrs. Sharp read:

Clean laundry. So welcome. We laughed out loud and the guards heard us, so no food yesterday and today. How I long for a slice of sky.

"When I was younger," she told Thomas, "I was sure she meant 'pie.' I didn't think you could have desires other than food if it was kept from you for days on end. And pie is my favorite. But I've learned since that there are many other things that can sustain you. For Nora, who was fed by nature, to not see the sky for days on end, well, that was a form of torture. Prisoners are often deprived of light, you see."

A strange thought came into Thomas's head, and before he could think to examine it, it came out of his mouth. "Did my mother feed the birds when she was visiting you?"

"Sometimes she did. She was very good at keeping still."

Thomas returned the note and the magnifying glass to Mrs. Sharp, who put them in her pocket. "Did she see this?"

"I told her this story, too, once when we were talking about her . . . condition. She had compared it to a sort of prison, you see, and that's when I brought the note out. Now . . ."

She instructed Thomas to reach out his arms. Depositing a handful of seeds in his outstretched palm, Mrs. Sharp stood behind him, waiting. "Hold still, Thomas," she instructed. "I see one of my favorites and he's a fearless thing . . ."

It wasn't long before a chickadee came to rest on the tips of his glove. He was so light. Thomas remained very still as the bird regarded him, turning its head to see him fully with its shiny black eye. Reaching in, it took a sunflower kernel before flying off to the safety of a tree branch.

"I did it," Thomas whispered.

"Yes, you did. But now . . ." Mrs. Sharp untied the apron and brushed the hair out of his eyes. "You need to go home. In time the answers will come to you."

"Maybe if I could come here . . . and be still and feed the birds . . . the answers would come."

"You can wait for permission to do that," Mrs. Sharp said. "Or you can act now. Remember, Thomas, conditions are rarely ideal."

"What I still don't understand is why none of the animals in the story can talk." Thomas stared at the birds as they lifted and settled. "The polar bear did once, but the pony doesn't talk...I can't talk. There's something wrong with all of us."

"Wrong? Or broken? If broken, can you be mended? That is the question."

"I have another question."

"Ask it, dear."

"Was it you who sent me the Revolutionnaire?"

"Yes."

"Why? Why did you do that?"

"I thought it might help you to remember happier times with your mother. Now, go into the powder room and wash your face. Then put on your socks and shoes. It's getting late."

In the bathroom, Thomas looked at himself in the mirror after he'd rinsed his tearstained face. He was so pale. He felt like Nora, in desperate need of a slice of sky.

Chapter 36

Back home, he closed the door, careful to turn the handle so it wouldn't make a sound; but his father heard anyway.

"Thomas, is that you back from Giselle's?" His father came up the stairs toward him. "Did Martin's mother come pick him up?"

Thomas nodded, hoping it was true.

"While you were gone, Officer Grant came by to...just to check on us...see how we were doing..."

Thomas looked up at his father, who turned away. He was concealing something.

"I said we were fine, of course."

Thomas waited.

"There is something else. She found a...Well, I should probably just show you. She asked me to keep it. I don't know why I agreed. It was imprudent of me." Mr. Moran headed back down the basement stairs.

Dave fluttered his wings. Thomas's father didn't keep things for no reason, and he looked so pained when he mentioned it that Thomas was certain this could not be anything good.

Mr. Moran returned with the brown box the Revolutionnaire had been delivered in. It was turned on its side and Thomas could see a big hole had been cut out of what was now the top.

"What is that on the back of your head?" his father asked as Thomas leaned over. "It looks like bird poop."

Thomas brought his hand to his head.

"Don't touch it. I'll get a washcloth." He set the box on the floor.

Inside the box was a cat. Not a kitten, but not a full-grown cat either. Something in between. Like he was. Stroking the cat's fur with the back of his finger, Thomas noticed the little cat was all black except for white paws and whiskers.

His father returned with the washcloth; leaning over Thomas, he cleaned his son's hair. "Someone brought this little guy to the police station. They found him outside—in this weather—and, well, Officer Grant said it wasn't uncommon for people to drop off animals. The police officers call animal control when that happens, but . . ."

Thomas focused on petting the cat as Mr. Moran explained. He couldn't understand why his father had agreed to take the cat, especially when he didn't want to. Mrs. Sharp said not everything could be saved. But Officer Grant and his father had proven that this cat, at least, could be.

"The shelter is full," his father explained. "You know, where they try to find lost animals a home. Officer Grant already has four cats. She said her boyfriend..."

Thomas turned around. He wanted to see the look on his father's face. Other people's problems didn't concern them. They had enough problems of their own.

"I...I...She told me it was actually her daughter who suggested it."

Lily. She makes the butterfly hair clips.

"It occurred to me that it might help. With you. With... the talking."

Reaching into his back pocket, Thomas pulled out his notepad. "Will you let me visit Mrs. Sharp?" he wrote before holding it up to his father.

"Does it matter what I say?" Thomas's father kneaded the skin above his eyes. "I'm guessing you were there today helping with the birds."

Thomas chewed the end of his pen.

"About the talking," he wrote. "I think I'm getting better and I'm glad you took the cat. We could call him Boots."

"Okay." Mr. Moran pushed the hair away from Thomas's forehead and looked into his son's eyes, but Thomas couldn't read his expression.

Chapter 37

Now that Thomas had seen what an awful mess could be made of a story, he built a roaring fire for his mother and left her and the pony beside it. He had the bear join them, too, and his mother had pulled them close so the bear's fur coat could warm them all.

From his perch on a craggy outcropping, Thomas watched over his mother, feeling as he had so many times before—not at all sure what to do. Maybe he would keep her there forever, staring into the fire and warming her hands.

In the middle of February, after a deep snowfall, Thomas saw his father shoveling Mrs. Sharp's sidewalk. "It's not like I harbor any ill will toward her," Thomas heard his father tell Aunt Sadie as they talked on the phone. "I did it last year."

And Mr. Moran had invited Ms. Dover and Giselle for dinner the following evening. He'd told Aunt Sadie he was getting on with his life. "You're moving on with yours, obviously."

Thomas wasn't sure what this meant exactly, but he suspected it had something to do with Mr. Walters. He suspected because Aunt Sadie knew things about him that he hadn't told them during cooking lessons. She knew he played mid-forward in high school when he'd only told them about playing in college. And that his father spent months away from the family on an Alaskan fishing boat.

As they made their way down the international aisle of the grocery store his father said, "Hmmm," more than once. They'd agreed to make Mexican food, since most people liked it. Now they stood, side by side, gazing at the enormous selection of taco shells, salsa, even canned cactus.

"What do you think?" his father said finally. "Should we make something vegetarian? They seem like vegetarians to me." Mr. Moran had grown used to answering himself. "Vegetarian is the safe bet," he decided.

Thomas noticed that his father was presuming again.

His father picked up a can of refried beans, which didn't look very delicious to Thomas. "This might do," his father murmured, holding the can away from him and reading the label. "Easy bean enchiladas."

Having a recipe and instructions seemed to cheer his father, who kept strolling down the aisle, looking for ingredients. Picking up a bag of tortillas, he said, "Someone needs to explain to me the difference between corn and flour tortillas.

His father consulted the side of the can of beans again. "It doesn't specify."

If only there were a *Chicago Manual of Style* for tortillas, Thomas thought.

"Excuse me." His father turned to face a woman with a cart filled with groceries.

"Can you tell me, for this recipe, should I purchase corn or flour tortillas? Furthermore, how large should they be?"

Thomas noticed the woman eyeing their empty cart before taking the can from his father.

"It really depends on what you like best," she said, looking at the recipe on the can. "Flour is . . . smoother. But for this recipe? I prefer corn. It has more tooth.

"These will do," she said, plucking a package from the pile. "Though I'd advise more beans."

Shifting from one foot to the other, Thomas rubbed his arms, imagining his father thinking that what you *liked* and what *will do* weren't rules at all.

"That's great," his father said. "Thank you."

At home, Thomas's father clipped the recipe off the can label and taped it to the cupboard above the sink. He washed his hands. Thomas washed his hands, too, and waited for directions. They stood there, facing each other, his father in his mother's apron, a big spoon in his hand. Thomas with his arms empty. Waiting.

Waiting for what?

Thomas didn't know. There was no past behavior on which to judge this moment. He and his father were in new territory.

Directions, then? Not so much for the easy bean enchiladas, but for life. Every day of it. For the last couple of years Helen and her moods were what gave them direction. What would shape their days now? What would tell them if this was a good day or a bad day?

"Son," his father began, "would you mind if I made this on my own? It says it's easy..."

Thomas shrugged; he turned to go to his room.

"Maybe you could...set the dining room table? Do you think we should have candles? For the company?"

When he'd finished setting the table, Thomas tore a piece of aluminum foil from the roll, scrunched it up, and tied it to a ribbon he found in his mother's desk drawer. As soon as the shiny ball appeared in Boots's range of vision, he came alive, rolling onto his back, paws jabbing at the air like a prizefighter. If he managed to snag it with a claw and pull it into his mouth, Boots let it go again, clearly preferring the chase. Thomas obliged him until he could think of no more flight patterns. Then he got out the brush his father had purchased at the pet store and stroked the cat's side, causing him to purr like a tiny, well-oiled engine. When he reached the cat's neck, Boots licked Thomas's finger with his sandy tongue. Thomas wondered if there was any chance his father would let him sleep with Boots. He thought it might even be worth sleeping on the kitchen floor if he could lie next to this warm purring body and rub his cheek against Boots's silky fur.

At precisely 6:15, Thomas's father removed the recipe for easy bean enchiladas that he'd underscored in his red highlighter pen and slipped it into one of Helen's cookbooks. Taking off his apron, he looked over the table Thomas had set.

"Why did you use the juice glasses?" he asked.

Thomas shrugged. He knew the decision would trouble his father. After all, it was dinner. But Thomas thought it looked better to have four glasses the same rather than mis-matched ones.

"Thomas, these are cocktail napkins."

Normally they used squares of paper towel, but Thomas had found these in the buffet.

"Oh well," his father said. "The red looks nice. Did you brush your teeth?"

Thomas had brushed his teeth that morning, as he always did. Were you supposed to brush them again when people came for dinner?

His father left him wondering as he disappeared up the stairs.

Thomas felt a little flutter in his tummy and sat down on

the bottom step, facing the front door. He inhaled slowly, realizing that this was a good feeling. A fizzy feeling...like Dave slurping up nectar from the floor of his stomach.

There was a knock on the door and Thomas stood, expecting a burst of Ms. Dover and Giselle, air kisses and bouncy hair; but instead, he answered the door to Mrs. Sharp, holding a bag of kitty-licious treats.

"Thomas, dear. Giselle told me about Boots and I thought—"

Thomas's father came down the stairs. "Amalia?"

"Mr. Moran, forgive me. I just came by to give these to Thomas and to thank you for clearing my—"

"Amalia, what a nice surprise!" Ms. Dover came up behind Mrs. Sharp, interrupting her thank-you speech. "I didn't know you were joining us."

Over the next sixty seconds, a great deal of heat was lost from the Morans' house.

"Oh, no. I've interrupted..." Mrs. Sharp held out the bag of kitty treats. "I'll just be on my way."

Everyone looked at Mr. Moran, who should have been making a decision, but who seemed—at that moment—to be lost. In the brief stillness, the thought occurred to Thomas that this was the time to help with *his* father's story. So he put his arms around his father's waist and hugged him. Tight.

"Of course, of course," his father said, pulling Thomas in closer and hugging him back. "I...meant to call. Really. Come in. You must stay. And please. Call me Brian."

"Yes, you should stay." Ms. Dover put her arm around Mrs. Sharp's waist. "I've brought enough sangria for a crowd." She held up a pitcher filled with fruit and what looked like cranberry juice.

"I have the kids' version." Giselle clasped another pitcher to her chest. "But it will freeze if I don't get inside."

Everyone moved inside and Ms. Dover supervised the re-setting of the table. A red tablecloth was found in the buffet and another juice glass. And a bowl for the tortilla chips.

After they were seated, Mr. Moran passed the chips to Thomas, who looked into his father's eyes and quietly said, "Thank you," ending almost seven weeks of silence with his father and turning the page to the next chapter.

Chapter 38

The next morning, while the toaster ticked away the seconds, Thomas peeked into the dining room to see what remained of the evening before. He knew the red tablecloth was in the washer, that the dishes had been cleaned and the candles had been put away, but he wondered if there was something left, something invisible, like the scents that dogs found at the base of a tree.

He still felt full. Stepping into the room, he rested his fingers on Giselle's chair.

"Did Mrs. Moran like Mexican food?" Giselle had asked. Not "does" but "did."

His father shook his head. "Nothing too spicy for Helen," he'd said.

Now his father called him back into the kitchen for breakfast.

"Nadine said it was her turn next." Thomas picked up the

piece of toast on his plate, but he did not bite into it. "When will that be?"

"I don't know, Thomas." His father reached over and squeezed his arm. "Eat your toast."

Thomas took a small bite to please his father. "Can we invite Aunt Sadie and Mr. Walters next time? And Martin?"

"This is beginning to sound like a birthday party."

It was still winter. Thomas's birthday wasn't until April.

"Do we have to wait until it's my birthday?"

"You're full of questions this morning." His father smiled as he said this. Thomas knew the smile was for the talking. He wasn't sure if it was for the questions, too.

For some reason, Thomas thought of the time he first went to Giselle's house the day she said she needed to assess him.

"Do you like jokes?" he asked his father.

"Not typically." His father had finished his toast.

"Are you happy?" Thomas asked him.

Mr. Moran put his coffee mug on his toast plate and folded the paper towel square so that he could use the clean side at the next meal. "I don't know what happy is, Thomas. But your talking to me is the closest I've felt to happy in a long time." He squeezed Thomas's arm a second time.

"What if we want to have more than six at the table? Aunt Sadie and Mr. Walters makes seven. And Martin makes eight."

"We do have a leaf, Thomas." His father patted the seat next to him. "I want to ask you something. I... I'm thinking about organizing a small service. For your mother. To remember her. It's called a memorial service."

"Like a church service?" Thomas didn't understand why they needed a service to remember her when he remembered her every time he looked at her chair in the kitchen.

"Not exactly. It's something you do when someone has … left. It provides closure."

Thomas shook his head. "What is closure?"

"It's like … an end to something. Officer Grant gave me a business card when your mom disappeared. It's for a place where people go who have a family member who suffers or suffered with depression. Well, I've been going there … to the meetings. On Thursdays. While you are at school. And someone in the group suggested it. To get closure. Come here, son. Are you too big to sit on my lap?"

Thomas couldn't remember the last time he'd sat on his father's lap. Certainly it wasn't since he'd grown an inch as measured by his father against the door frame on his last birthday.

His father reached out his arms and Thomas let himself be drawn in. Then Thomas asked the same question he'd asked Mrs. Sharp. "She's dead, isn't she?"

"Oh, Thomas," he said. "It's true that I place great importance on what can be verified. That's my job. If your mother had died in a car accident, for example, then we would know unquestionably that she was …" Shifting his weight, Thomas's father rearranged Thomas's legs so that they draped over the side of his lap. "That she was gone from us. But I do believe she is and I know she loved us. And she did everything in her power—" He broke off to lean back so that he and Thomas could look each other in the eye. "To stay."

"She said she would write me." Thomas bit his lip. "I believed her."

"I'm sure she meant to write, son. The important thing to remember is that she couldn't make decisions like a healthy person. She—" His father stopped talking and Thomas thought it might be because he was afraid that his voice would get quivery.

Thomas waited for his father to finish, but there was nothing his father could add.

"Would you like to read your story to me? The one you and Mrs. Sharp were working on?"

"But...you said..."

"I've been thinking a lot about that story, Thomas. Sometimes I'm wrong. The people in my group thought it was a good idea. In fact, everyone but me—Nadine, your aunt—"

"It's not done yet. I...I might need your help," Thomas continued. "As long as you remember that it's my story."

"I don't write stories, Thomas. I am a copy editor."

"But you change them, don't you?"

His father nodded. "I do sometimes change them. But just for clarity."

"You changed the story last night," Thomas said. "When you invited Mrs. Sharp to stay for dinner."

Thomas's father helped his son back to the floor and stood up, signaling that the conversation was over. "I suppose I did," he said.

"And it wasn't just for clarity," Thomas added.

His father turned and went down the basement steps, letting Thomas have the last word.

Chapter 39

On the third Saturday in March, the day before Helen's memorial service, Aunt Sadie picked up the prep cooks—Thomas and Giselle—while Mr. Walters stayed back at her apartment ensuring *mise en place*. This, according to Giselle, meant everything in its place.

"French chefs insist on having all the ingredients prepared before cooking begins," she told them. Pausing in the hall outside Aunt Sadie's apartment, Giselle began to snap her fingers. "Does Mr. Walters have...Is that salsa music he's playing, Sadie?"

"Apparently, it is..." Aunt Sadie replied, glancing over her shoulder at Mr. Sampson's apartment door before adding quietly, "Without regard for the neighbors."

The music spilled out of the apartment door as they opened it, greeting them noisily. Hurrying the children inside, Aunt Sadie struggled to pull off her boots. "Jason, turn it down!

Coats over here," she instructed Thomas and Giselle. "Shoes on the plastic mat."

They could hear Mr. Walters in the kitchenette, singing to the music as water splashed into the sink.

"*¡Hola, hola, bienvenidos a mi casa!*" He bowed to Aunt Sadie. "Well . . . your *casa*," he said. "And you must be Giselle."

"Hi, Mr. Walters. Do you dance salsa?" Giselle placed one hand on her stomach and waved the other in the air, dancing her imaginary partner to the other side of the kitchen.

"I do," he said.

"What happened here?" Aunt Sadie gazed at her kitchenette, where the countertops were filled with bottles and cans Thomas had never seen before—not even in a grocery store.

"You can't cook on an empty stomach, so I made us a Korean hot pot."

Using her remote to turn down the music, Aunt Sadie surveyed the mess around them. "I thought . . ." was all she could manage. "What happened to 'everything in its place'?"

"A little mess is the sign of an accomplished cook, Sadie. Everything will be in its place by the time we leave. Now . . ." He gestured toward the stove. "A good restaurant staff takes time for a family meal. So. I've got buckwheat noodles here, a little mandu for—"

"Man what?" Giselle wanted to know.

"They're stuffed dumplings. You'll love them. I'm guessing you know your way around a pair of chopsticks, Giselle?"

Mr. Walters put a white towel over his arm and laid a pair of chopsticks on them.

Giselle nodded, took a pair, and clicked them together. "They're pretty. I've never seen metal ones. Can I try?" she asked, motioning in the direction of a bubbling pot on the stove.

"The noodles aren't quite done yet, which gives us time for—" Mr. Walters broke off, grabbing the remote and raising the volume on the music. "A brief interlude," he said, sliding across the kitchen floor and singing in Spanish to the music before shouting: "It's fusion night at the Torinis'!"

"It will be night if we don't step it up here." Aunt Sadie was not pleased.

Dancing his way back to the pot, Mr. Walters said: "A watched pot doesn't simmer, Sadie."

"But it is simmering."

"*And* the timer is on." Mr. Walters took hold of Aunt Sadie's hands and tried to get her to dance with him, but she wasn't having it. Instead, she tore some sheets from the paper towel roll and began wiping the counter.

Everyone got quiet then and watched the pot simmer. Soon they were sitting at the table, their chopsticks in hand, looking down at the noodles and dumplings. Rolling an impressive ball of noodles around his chopsticks, Mr. Walters popped them into his mouth.

Thomas had no idea what he said next. Maybe that the noodles were delicious?

When Aunt Sadie used her napkin to wipe up the broth that dripped from Mr. Walters's noodles, he grabbed her hand again. "You must try this, Miss Torini, or you are missing out. Here." Before she could object, Mr. Walters had twirled another clump of noodles onto his chopsticks and sent them, dripping, over to Aunt Sadie's mouth.

The look on her face made Thomas think that Mr. Walters was on the verge of joining the ranks of Mr. Montgomery, her boss. Mr. Walters must have seen the look, too, because he said, "You could try being a bit more adventurous, Sadie."

Aunt Sadie's mouth stayed closed; the noodles dangled, dripping more broth onto the table. "I am trying," she said as she left the kitchen and went into her bedroom.

Mr. Walters sighed and dropped the noodles back into his bowl. "Eat up, everyone. Then we'll get this cleaned up so we can start cooking for tomorrow."

After he'd put most of his exotic bottles back into a box he'd brought with him, Mr. Walters wiped down the counters and left to find Aunt Sadie.

"They're fighting," Giselle said after she'd ventured down the hall to listen at the bedroom door. "I'm guessing we have a Pisces and Virgo here."

When they returned, Aunt Sadie seemed calmer. She opened a bag she'd brought out with her and began handing out aprons. "I snagged these at Value Village," she told them.

Thomas took his but didn't put it on. "I'll wear my old one," he said.

"Your old one is too small, Thomas," Aunt Sadie said. "I gave it back to your dad. See? I have a new one, too."

All of a sudden, there was Dave again, scaling the sides of Thomas's stomach. Where was his old apron? Would his father give it to Goodwill? Helen had sewn that apron for Thomas. At his request, she'd sewn a special loop on the front—to hold his wooden spoon. That was before, of course. Before the baby. Before the medicine bottles and the rooms with drawn curtains and the leaking tears.

Sometimes it was hard to remember before Baby Sadie; sometimes it was even hard to remember before Helen leaving. The old apron had connected Thomas and his mother— what would connect them now? Would new things keep being added over the old things so that someday he wouldn't remember anything about her at all?

Of course, no one else thought about this; they were tying on their new aprons. Giselle had chosen a green one covered in chili peppers.

"Thomas," Mr. Walters said, breaking into his thoughts. "Since you're now so familiar with the operation of the Rev-olutionnaire, I suggest that you be chief food processor." Mr. Walters handed Sadie a knife he'd pulled from his box. "This is my chef's knife, Sadie. I'm trusting you with its care for the cucumber slices. And, Giselle. Hmmm...let's see..."

Mr. Walters took Giselle's hand and twirled her. Then, putting his other hand around her waist, he began danc-ing with her in the kitchen. "Queen of salsa," Mr. Walters announced, twirling her again and dipping her back so that her hair skimmed the floor.

"Where'd you learn to do that?" Aunt Sadie asked Giselle.

"My mom and I took lessons," Giselle said. "Usually I lead." Hugging Mr. Walters, she bestowed him with air kisses before whispering to Thomas, "It's so nice to have a partner who can really dance—don't tell my mom!"

Mr. Walters grabbed a scrap of paper from the counter and held it up. "Here's the menu *du jour*," he said. "We're serving your mom's favorite foods, Thomas, so I've got potatoes au gratin, cucumber sandwiches with watercress, and pecan Sadies."

"Pecan Sadies? Did Helen invent those for you?" Giselle asked Aunt Sadie.

"They're pecan sandies," Aunt Sadie explained. "But Helen changed the name for me. She's made them for us since we were..."

Thomas caught the mistake the same moment that Aunt Sadie did. She did not say Helen *used* to make them, but that she did make them, as if Helen would stop by in a little while and show them how to do it.

Aunt Sadie sat down in a kitchen chair, turning so she faced the cupboards.

Mr. Walters switched off the music and sat next to her. "I hate when that happens... You just got lost in the taste of those cookies, didn't you?" he asked, putting his hand over hers.

"But Mrs. Sharp said the sense memories are the best," Thomas said.

"When you've lost someone you love, Thomas, you understand that the best and the worst feelings can happen at the same time."

"Did you lose someone you love, Mr. Walters?" Giselle asked. "Is that how you know?"

Mr. Walters nodded. He squeezed Aunt Sadie's hand. "Do you mind if I tell them?"

Aunt Sadie shook her head, keeping her head down.

"I lost my brother," Mr. Walters continued. "I was away at med school. He was still in high school. One Saturday night, he and his friends were horsing around in a pickup truck. His buddy didn't know he was standing in the back and gunned the truck. My brother fell off the back and hit his head. And he died."

"That's terrible."

"I know. But it happened and I can't change it. What's strange is that I feel like now I have to live life for both of us."

"What happened to medical school?" Giselle asked Mr. Walters.

"I dropped out to walk the Camino de Santiago," Mr. Walters said. "It's a pilgrim's walk in Spain. We were going to do it together when he graduated. I started walking and... I just haven't stopped yet, I guess."

Mr. Walters looked around, surprised. "How did we get on this subject?"

"I asked you," Giselle said, giving Mr. Walters another hug. "In French, we say: *Je vous adresse mes sinceres condoléances*. It means, please accept my most sincere condolences. We had a whole session on expressions of sympathy in Saturday school."

"It sounds better in French, but the hug feels good in any language, right, Sadie?"

"Right." Aunt Sadie put her arms around Giselle putting her arms around Mr. Walters.

"Come here, Thomas. I could use a hug from you, too," his aunt said.

"And then it's time to start cooking," Mr. Walters said.

While Giselle and Sadie cut cucumbers and thin slices of rye for the sandwiches, Mr. Walters showed Thomas how to cut the peeled potatoes to fit into the feed tube of the food processor.

"We need uniform slices," Mr. Walters explained, "so the gratin cooks evenly. Thomas?" Mr. Walters leaned in so that only Thomas could hear what he was about to say. "That story you are making...with your mom in it. Sadie told me about it. Could you explain to me how you do that? I have nieces and nephews who will never know my brother unless—"

"What was his name?" Thomas asked.

"Andrew."

"That's a good name."

"I know. I keep having the same dream every few months. Pretty much since he died. Andrew's with our old retriever, Misty. My sister, Renee, insists that he was too young to remember when we had Misty—"

"It doesn't matter what Renee thinks," Thomas said. "It's

your dream." Thomas put a piece of potato into the feed tube, pressed the food pusher against it, and pushed the button on the processor.

"They're in the barn behind our house," Mr. Walters continued when the machine had finished. "It's an old barn. We didn't use it, but...in my dream, they live there—Andrew and Misty. In the hayloft. It's like a cave."

Mr. Walters was seeing that hayloft now. Thomas could tell because, just like when Helen went somewhere far off in her mind, his eyes were directed at the cupboard over Thomas's head.

"I go out there at night, climb into the hayloft, and shine my flashlight. There's just this small entrance woven all around with hay. It's like an animal's nest. Andrew waves for me to come in, but something, maybe my weight, causes the whole thing to collapse.

"We all fall. It doesn't hurt because there is hay all around. Sometimes I hear barking in the distance. Then that's it. That's when I wake up."

"You should start the story there," Thomas said quietly. "Maybe not when you wake up, but when Andrew does."

"Really?"

"He fell, didn't he? But instead of falling off the truck, this time he falls into the hay." Unlatching the processor lid, Thomas scooped out perfectly uniform slices of potato. "Maybe he fell into a magic place in the astral plane. But it's just a suggestion," he remembered to add. "Only if it feels right to you."

"Well," Mr. Walters said, "Misty is definitely going to be with him in my story."

Thomas nodded, thinking of his fox. "If you can't stop thinking about her, Misty has to be there."

"Thank you, Thomas. Can I show it to you? When I've got something down on paper?"

"Of course."

Chapter 40

When Helen disappeared, people came and dropped off food and left. They did not come and stay. To stay would have required them to talk, and what was there to say? She had vanished. Aunt Sadie once told Thomas that on the east and west coasts people talked about the traffic when they didn't know what to say; but in the Midwest where Michigan was, they talked about the weather. After Helen went missing—because she disappeared when it was so cold outside—it wasn't even safe to talk about the weather.

That's why Thomas's father told him on the morning of his mother's memorial service that there weren't likely to be a lot of people. A lot of people had loved Helen, he assured Thomas. But there weren't all that many who would feel comfortable attending a service like the one they were having.

"Who will be here?" Thomas wondered.

"For sure? The Templetons, the Dovers, Mrs. Sharp, Officer

Grant...a few people from the bank, the day care center, and the community college who helped us search."

"Is Grandma Moran coming?"

Mr. Moran shook his head. "Her health is not good, Thomas. Aunt Priscilla will bring her when..."

Thomas didn't prompt his father, because he knew from listening through the cold air register that Aunt Priscilla and Grandma Moran would come when there was a funeral. A funeral happened when you had a body.

"Have you decided which tie to wear?" his father asked now, opening his closet door.

Thomas had decided. The blue one.

His father arranged the tie under Thomas's collar before handing him a sheet of paper. "It's the order of the service," his father explained. "The story you created about your mother will be at the end."

It was only fifteen minutes to "go time," as Aunt Sadie liked to say, and yet it was very quiet downstairs. As he grabbed the stair rail to get a glimpse of people arriving, Thomas noticed his wrists poking out of his Sunday suit. He tugged at his sleeves; Dave also seemed to be making last-minute adjustments.

Thomas watched as his father took people's coats, and Aunt Sadie shook hands and directed guests to the living room, where they'd set up the folding chairs the night before. The Templetons arrived just before Officer Grant came in, holding a child's hand.

"It's Lily . . . the one who made the butterfly clip," Thomas told Dave.

"And the reason we have Boots," Dave reminded Thomas.

Now came Ms. Dover and Giselle in her purple jacket and a black velvet headband Thomas had never seen before. Mrs. Sharp arrived in her yellow rain boots.

"Thomas?" his father called up.

It was time to go down.

"How handsome you look!" Ms. Dover cupped Thomas's chin in her hands before Giselle could steal him away for air kisses.

"I'll be sitting in front with Martin," Giselle whispered.

Officer Grant stepped up to shake Thomas's hand. "Hello, Thomas. This is my daughter, Lily."

"Can I see Boots?" Lily asked, regarding Thomas with wide gray eyes.

"Lily, I told you we could ask about Boots after."

"It's okay," Thomas said. "He'll be coming."

"Thank you, Thomas. We'll take a seat."

"Thomas?" Mrs. Sharp pulled off her scarf and handed it to Thomas to hold as she undid the buttons of her coat. "Are you ready?"

"I think so," he said, though he wasn't at all sure. Neither was Dave.

There was music playing in the living room and all of a sudden more people than chairs. Thomas could not fit the scene in front of him into anything from his memory. Here was another new picture to be laid over the top of their empty living room and drawn curtains.

"It's time to gather, everyone." Reverend Amanda clapped her hands together. "Find a seat, please. For those who are able, there are spaces on the floor up here."

"Getting down there isn't the problem," said Sadie's boss, Mr. Montgomery, grunting as he lowered himself to the ground.

Standing next to the fireplace, Reverend Amanda spoke in her church voice: "Welcome. At the request of Helen's family, this will be an informal service to honor the life of Helen Moran, a lovely, quiet presence among us. We'll begin with Helen's sister reading a poem."

Aunt Sadie stood up, but she did not go to the front of the room the way Mrs. Evans made her students do. She stood in her place next to Mr. Walters, who had his hand on her back.

"Helen loved this poem, 'Stopping by Woods on a Snowy Evening,' by Robert Frost," she said. "I'm sure she was thinking of it when she—" Aunt Sadie stopped and looked over the audience. She had the look of someone in a play who had botched their lines. Tucking her chin and looking at the ground, she said quietly to herself: "Just get on with it, Sadie."

Reading the poem seemed to get easier as she went along, describing the woods and how lovely they were, even though they were dark. Thomas pictured Mr. Frost trudging through them the way his mother did in his story as Aunt Sadie read the last line: "And miles to go before I sleep."

Thomas turned the words over in his mind. Could two people make the same story? He wondered if someone Mr. Frost knew had stepped out on a cold winter afternoon and not come back.

Or maybe it was Mr. Frost himself. But he must have come back. To write it down.

Mr. Moran, who'd been leaning against the wall by the fireplace, stepped forward and said, "I'm not much for public speaking, except if I'm teaching a class and talking about dangling modifiers." He paused while the English teachers laughed.

"Thomas and Sadie and I wanted to gather and remember Helen's life . . . There won't be a lot of sermonizing—forgive me, Amanda—but as you said, Helen was a quiet presence.

"It's why we've put out the photo albums. Helen loved her home. She loved watching the birds; she loved taking care of us—when she was able. Most of all, she loved being Thomas's mother. Much of the time—"

Mr. Moran broke off and looked out at those gathered, searching, until he'd caught Thomas's eye. "In recent years, of course . . . well, she couldn't do much. She was too sick. It's important to know if you haven't experienced a loved one with depression, that depression is a disease, an illness if you will, like any medical illness you can think of—cancer, heart disease, diabetes.

"Helen couldn't wish herself well with motivational pep talks or by watching funny movies or thinking positive thoughts. Thomas and Sadie and I did what we could to help her recover. She would have if she could. I know that. She tried hard to stay with us."

Though Mr. Moran was speaking loud enough for everyone to hear, his eyes had not left Thomas.

Thomas nodded to show he understood.

"Our friend Amalia helped Thomas create a story about Helen, and in a moment they are going to read it to you, but first if you get out that sheet of paper I put on your seat, we're going to sing this hymn together. It was a favorite of Helen's. She said it reminded her of peace—the idea that there might be, at the same time, peace all over the world."

Reverend Amanda stepped forward and sang a note. A few people sang the note back. "I'll hum the first stanza so you get the melody and then I'll invite you to join in." She looked at Thomas's father. "All right?"

He nodded.

Thomas closed his eyes for the humming; Helen used to hum the song while she did the dishes. The minister's humming didn't sound like Helen's humming, which had been soft and blended in with the splashing water.

Now people joined in the singing, but Thomas didn't want to sing. He wanted to do what he was good at—listen. So that's what he did, listened as the others sang about a beautiful country where the heart resides. And he wondered if that could mean the land where Helen was now, even though it was a place not found on any map.

Other hearts. Other lands. Thomas let the words wash over him. A long silence followed the end of the singing, which was then followed by a rustling of searching through pockets for tissues. Even Mr. Montgomery blinked away a tear, rubbing the side of his face.

Dave stretched, sweeping his wings across the sides of Thomas's stomach.

Here we go.

Chapter 41

Stepping forward once again, Thomas's father said, "Amalia? Can we get you a chair?"

"That would be lovely," she said.

A chair was passed overhead, and when she was seated Mrs. Sharp looked at Thomas, who came forward as well, even though he would rather have stayed in his place as Aunt Sadie did. He took a deep breath and willed Dave to settle. This was for his mother, after all.

His father put a stool next to Mrs. Sharp's chair and Thomas sat down on it.

"When I first heard about Thomas's story," Mr. Moran said, "I was very much against it. I felt it would keep Thomas from understanding what had happened. But I've come to realize it was Thomas's unique way of keeping Helen close, and I . . . well . . ." Mr. Moran cleared his throat. "I'm proud of you, son."

Mrs. Sharp stood and gave Thomas's father a hug. After they'd both sat down, she looked first at Thomas, then out at those gathered.

"When Helen first disappeared," Mrs. Sharp began, "it was a very distressing time for her family. So...Thomas and I created a story. We put Helen into it. You must understand that, though I wrote it down for him, Thomas directed the story. He has a very strong imagination, I must say. This is one of the best stories I've ever read." Mrs. Sharp placed her hand on Thomas's knee, and gave him a smile. "And I've read my share. As Thomas worked on his story, I was reminded that it's not just characters who must be brave, but the authors, too.

"Thomas waded in...You were afraid, weren't you, Thomas?"

Thomas nodded. He'd been very afraid. Dave nodded, too.

"But you kept on going, even when all seemed lost. It's what we hope for most when it's our turn to be brave. Isn't that right?"

There was nodding and agreement.

"So..." Mrs. Sharp opened the folder in her lap, straightened her shoulders, readying herself. "Shall we begin?"

"You can close your eyes if you want," Thomas said softly to the audience from his seat next to Mrs. Sharp. "It helps me...sometimes...to go there."

Everyone listened to Thomas and closed their eyes. Except Giselle, who held Boots in her lap, stroking him. She waited until she made eye contact with Thomas and sent him a kiss through the air.

Mrs. Sharp began to read about Helen in her car, about Helen meeting the polar bear and the old woman in the hut. She got all the way to the part where things looked their worst; where the bear, the pony, and Helen sat for what seemed like an endless amount of time, warming themselves by the fire.

She paused there—just for a moment—wondering if this was the spot where Thomas wanted to pick up reading.

He shook his head. It sounded better to him when she read it. He closed his eyes, too, so he could stay with his mother just a little longer.

Mrs. Sharp continued to read:

Thomas—the owl—sat on his perch on the craggy out-cropping high above the fire, peering down at Helen, the pony, and the bear. They'd been there so long.

Helen looked up at Thomas and said: "It's time, but there must be three. Thomas, I need your swift wings. Can you find the fox and bring him back to me?"

Thomas circled the fire once, twice, stretching his wings before setting off.

Flying over rivers covered in ice and forests covered in snow, he spied the fox, finally, at the edge of a small clearing. As he landed nearby, it seemed to Thomas that the fox was dead. So very still. But not yet. Small puffs of steam came from his nostrils.

He was so weak the fox could barely lift his head, let alone defend himself against the talons of a great owl. Thomas hopped over to the fox, whose eyes followed him, but that was all. Pinching the ruff of fur at the fox's neck with his beak, he flapped his powerful wings and lifted them both into the air.

The fox was nothing to carry. Guided by memory, Thomas reached the bonfire just as dawn was approaching.

"Oh, Thomas. Thank you!" Helen said, gathering the fox into her arms and cradling him like a baby. She placed him with the pony and the polar bear by the fire.

As Thomas settled once again on his perch, the polar bear queen appeared.

"You found the three, Helen," she said in her deep voice. "Well done. Are you ready now?"

Gazing fondly at her son, Helen replied: "I am. Are you ready, Thomas?"

Thomas blinked his great owl eyes. He was ready, though for what he did not know.

Helen moved to the pony, kneeling beside her and running her finger over the ridges of her ribs. "Sadie," she whispered, putting her arms around the pony's neck and rubbing her muzzle. Turning to the polar bear queen, she said: "Now let Sadie be Sadie."

The pony stretched her long neck and attempted to stand. Thomas could see the alarm in her brown eyes. "It won't hurt," Helen whispered. "It's meant to stop the hurting."

Then Helen saw her sister and embraced her tear-fully. They stayed just like this for some time until Helen unclasped Sadie's arms from around her and turned and knelt beside the little fox.

"You will go...and comfort them."

Kissing the top of the fox's head, Helen nodded to the polar bear queen and took a step back. The fox was no lon-ger a fox, but a cat uncurling itself into a long luxurious stretch.

Helen stroked the fur of Boots. "You will never be cold or afraid again. You've found your home." The little cat purred and licked Helen's finger with his sandy tongue.

Helen stood and turned to the bear. "You would have done anything to save me."

The wrinkled black bear bowed his neck.

"I know." Helen touched the scarred and worn skin, massaging the bear's back, caressing his face, tears flowing down her own.

"But I know my place is here now and you must go back." Breaking away, she added: "In time, you will heal." Helen looked at the polar bear queen once again.

Then Brian Moran stood before them. He was not stooped over; his eyes were not red from reading too many manuscripts. He stood straight, wearing the corduroy blazer that Helen had mended, his cheeks red from the cold.

Helen hugged him once more. Fiercely. "Good-bye, my love," she said.

Mrs. Sharp closed her folder and looked out at the audience. There was a long silence.

"That can't be the end," Aunt Sadie protested. "You haven't changed Thomas yet."

"I know it's your story, Thomas, but I don't understand." Giselle was trying to puzzle it through. "Helen's saved three things, but you're still an owl...How will you get back to being Thomas?"

"I think you must have skipped a part," Martin said.

"Martin's right, Thomas," Mr. Moran added. "We can't do this without you."

"All in good time..." Mrs. Sharp handed Thomas the folder. "Thomas, can you read the rest?"

Thomas took the folder from Mrs. Sharp, and they changed places so that he was sitting in the reading chair. He cleared his throat the way Principal Bowen did before she talked in a school assembly. Then he looked at the audience.

"This part is called 'Ever After,'" he said, and began to read.

"What about Thomas?" Brian Moran said. "He's coming back with us, isn't he?"

"Thomas is not under a spell anymore," Helen told her husband and her sister. "The spell is broken."

"There's just that one little problem that he's an owl instead of a boy," Sadie pointed out.

"Yes, he is," Helen agreed. "When he wants to be."

"You'll have to be clearer," Brian said.

"When there are further adventures, he will be an owl. Otherwise, he'll be the Thomas you know. A normal boy."

"But...isn't the story...over?" Sadie was looking down at herself. She had on her tracksuit. Just as if she were about to step on the treadmill.

"Helen, please." Brian took his wife's hand again. "You can't stay here like this either," he pleaded with her. "It's too cold. Even with that fur, you can't...you can't survive in this cold weather."

"No, I can't." Helen looked at him the way she did sometimes from her place at the kitchen table. As if she wished things weren't the way they were. "But this is where I belong and where Thomas can find me again in his stories."

Then she went over and put her hand on the polar bear queen's arm. "I'm ready to change so that I can stay here with you on the astral plane."

Snow began falling. It was so thick—as if a curtain separated Helen from her family.

The polar bear queen held out her paw. Suddenly the flurry ended and the sun shone on Helen, who was growing smaller and smaller, encased in glittering ice.

A silence fell over the group as threads of silver filled Helen's icy chrysalis, traveling up and down, contracting in some places and drawing inward, pushing out in others.

Like the pony and the fox and the bear before her, Helen was changing shape. When she'd become the size of an icicle that dangled from their eaves, the polar bear queen picked her up, gently enclosed her in both big paws, and breathed hot breaths so that the ice melted away.

Turning to the travelers, she extended her paw where a tiny figure unfolded itself. Brian and Sadie stepped closer. What at first appeared to be a giant snowflake was, in fact, two wings. As the lovely fragile creature perched on the claws of the polar bear queen unfurled her lacy wings, Thomas's family was seeing the very first snowflake butterfly.

It floated up, lighter than air, to rest on the same rock as Thomas.

And even though he was still an owl, Thomas could speak. Helen's transformation had broken the spell. She was all right now. She had a new life and a new shape and she could begin again—here with the polar bear queen. "The story is never over," Thomas told them. "Even a story that starts with good-bye."

Chapter 42

In the days following Helen's memorial service, Thomas kept to himself. It was hard to find things to do that seemed like the right things. His story with the polar bear queen was over and a new adventure had not yet begun. The space Dave had occupied in his stomach seemed empty and hollow, and when Thomas spoke to his butterfly there was no answer. Where was Dave now?

Maybe he should write a story that featured his butterfly. Maybe that would bring him back. Or maybe Dave had moved on and would not be back. Maybe he'd left to help some other boy.

On Saturday morning, Thomas was lying on his bed thinking about Dave and story ideas that just didn't seem ready to be stories when the doorbell rang.

"Thomas?" Giselle called up after his father had opened

the door. "I haven't seen you in almost a week. *Tu me manques.* I miss you."

Thomas slid off his bed and went downstairs.

"Can you come out for a minute? I want to show you something."

Thomas could feel a rush of warm air come through the open door; it was officially spring. He followed Giselle outside without putting on his coat.

She took him to the spot between their houses, near a tangle of bushes. "Here. This is what I wanted to show you."

"What do you call this?" Thomas lifted a soft, cream-colored bloom with his finger so he could see it more clearly.

"It's called a Lenten rose because it blooms in March, way before other flowers. See all these pretty pink speckles? My mom planted a purple one in our backyard, just for me." She breathed in noisily through her nose. "Don't you love the smell of spring?"

Thomas inhaled. He kneeled, poking his finger into the cold soil, he remembered that it was snowdrops his mother searched for in early spring.

"You never did, though, did you, Thomas?"

Thomas hadn't been paying close attention, so he wasn't sure what he'd never done. He asked Giselle to repeat what she'd just said.

"You never drew a picture of what I would look like if I were a butterfly."

Picking up a dead leaf, Thomas crumbled it on his lap. His knees were wet from the ground.

"It's okay if you didn't. I was just won—"

"You were too flat when I drew it," Thomas said. "So I cut it out instead."

"Like when we made snowflake butterflies? Can I see it? Please? I'll close my eyes and wait right here."

"You can only see it upstairs." Thomas stood up and walked back to the side door with Giselle following, chattering at him. They took off their shoes and put them on the plastic tray. Then he had Giselle follow him up the stairs, knowing that something was about to happen that would change UnderLand forever, just like his story had changed when he'd shared that with others.

"I'll need your help," he said, taking Giselle's shoulders and positioning her near the end of the bed. "Now, close your eyes and reach down until you feel the metal part of the bed. Good. Are your eyes closed still?"

Giselle nodded, pressing even tighter.

"Lift up the bed," Thomas instructed, standing on the other side and lifting at the same time. They stood his bed on its end, exposing the underside. His pillows and covers tumbled to the floor, the mattress started to buckle but was prevented from falling completely by the bed frame and wall.

"What are we doing?"

"Keep your eyes closed."

"I am. I am."

Thomas picked up the remote from his nightstand and pressed the on button for the Christmas lights. He moved the sweater boxes aside. Martin would need to make an accurate count, but Thomas guessed there was somewhere between one hundred and two hundred butterflies clinging to the metal mesh, softly lit by the white lights, their wings brushing against one another.

"Open your eyes," he said.

"Ooh, Thomas," Giselle cried out. "Are these all me?"

Thomas nodded.

Your dragonfly blouse, your sky-blue hair ribbon, the mossy green flecks in your eyes, the shiny purple of your jacket, the pink flush of your cheeks.

"It's a kaleidoscope," Thomas said.

"A kaleidoscope."

"That's what they call a bunch of butterflies."

"A whole bunch of butterflies." Giselle sank to her knees. "It's so perfect. How long have you been working on this?"

"Almost since..." Thomas thought back. It seemed like forever since he'd been snipping butterfly wings, and yet his mother had never seen them.

Has it really been forever? Forever since she left?

"I got the idea from Officer Grant," Thomas said. "She had one in her pocket when she came to tell us about the car."

"And these lights?"

"Aunt Sadie put those there at Christmas."

Sifting her hands through the snips of colored paper on the floor, Giselle asked: "Did you make them down here? Why is this one black over here?"

"It's not black. It's dark dark purple. That was for the day you bit Alexis."

"I see. That's for me when I'm angry. Just one? Oh, Thomas. You should see me at school. When Sandra imitates my French. Or last Tuesday when Alicia stole my dessert because she said I was getting too fat. I didn't bite her, though. If I do, I'll never get to the public middle school. And they have an orchestra. I could play my cello!"

Thomas nodded. "Should I make more? For all the times you're angry?" he asked her.

"No! I like that this is how you see me." Fingering a turquoise-blue wing with the letters "Happ" on it, Giselle looked up at Thomas. "This is how I want to be. Thank you, Thomas. *Je t'aime*. I love you! *C'est beau!* How beautiful! Can I take a picture to show my mom?"

Thomas thought that would be all right.

Giselle moved around the bed, looking for the best way to frame her photo.

After taking a few snapshots on her cell phone, Giselle examined the images. "Thomas," she said, her face flushing. "Do you know what this looks like? An art installation!"

Thomas did not know what an art installation was, though he could see the connection pleased Giselle very much. So much so that she looked it up on Wikipedia to show him.

"See?" she said, pressing her cheek to his as they examined the phone. "It's a site-specific, three-dimensional work. Of Giselle art!"

Having her own artwork made Giselle so happy she did a few salsa steps, catching Helen's coat beneath her foot and slipping to the floor.

"Thomas," she said after she'd righted herself. "Is this the coat..."

Thomas didn't have to say yes or no. Giselle knew the answer.

"Where did Helen get this coat?"

Thomas didn't know. "New-4-U?" he guessed.

"Do you know what this is?"

Thomas shrugged.

"Well, just look at the label. It's a Dior! This coat was made by a French designer."

Giselle held out the coat so that Thomas could look at the label.

But he did not see what she expected him to. That is, rather than focus on the long curled letters that spelled out Christian Dior, Thomas saw the label itself—the label that was stitched into the shiny lining of the coat.

Sewn on all sides but one, where the tiny stitches had been teased out.

Thomas was not seeing a label, but a mailbox. Thomas was remembering the story of the girl who longed for a slice of sky.

Of course, he wanted to stick his finger into the tiny opening but he resisted the urge. Thomas was good at waiting. Whatever was in there was not meant for Giselle, but for him.

His mother *had* written.

After they returned the coat to its place and lowered the bed back over it, Giselle said her good-byes. Thomas walked her down the stairs to the door and then walked back up the stairs. Sliding underneath the bed, he extracted a tiny folded sheet of paper from inside the label.

Dear Thomas, Remember this always, my love! 22:20–22:26.

Thomas crawled out of UnderLand and shouted for his father. He could hear him rushing from his office in response: into the kitchen and up the stairs.

"What is it, Thomas?" Mr. Moran said. "Are you all right?"

"She wrote!" Thomas shouted again, even though his father was right in front of him. "She *did* write to me. But... it's like Mrs. Sharp's journal about her father. I don't understand it."

"Is it...in another language?" Mr. Moran squinted at the slip of paper Thomas had handed over.

"No."

" 'Remember this always, my love! 22:20–22:26,' " his father read aloud. "Where did you get this, Thomas?"

Thomas explained that it had come from Helen's coat.

"The pocket of your mother's coat?"

His father was presuming again and Thomas did not correct him.

Mr. Moran rubbed his head, thinking. "It's so small, I must have missed it," he said finally. "This is so unlike your mother."

"Can we just imagine for a minute?" Thomas asked.

"Of course. You imagine."

Thomas took the paper back. He'd seen numbers like this somewhere before. Not these exact numbers, but...was it on a digital clock? Aunt Sadie's car had a digital clock. Martin wore a digital watch.

Where else?

"22:20–22:26," he whispered to himself.

For some reason, he thought of Mrs. Evans and how she liked to show them YouTube videos on her computer to clarify points she had made during Ask Mrs. Evans from channels like Braincraft and Talk Nerdy to Me.

He wasn't sure why he thought about that, so he stayed there for a minute, in the classroom, remembering a particular time when a girl with a British accent was explaining how blue morpho butterflies aren't really blue at all but only look blue in sunlight.

But this isn't about butterflies, is it?

No. It was something else. Thomas froze the image that appeared above Mrs. Evans's head. At one point George tipped his chair and fell backward and they had to put on the lights to make sure he didn't have a concussion. By the time they returned to the video, her computer had gone to sleep. She called up the channel once more.

"Where were we?" she asked after George was settled in the desk in the hall.

"Three twenty-two," Mary Mallender had said.

"Thank you, Mary," Mrs. Evans said, moving her cursor to 3:22 on the menu bar to continue the lesson. "It's nice to know someone is paying attention."

Thank you, Mary.

"I think I know what the numbers mean," Thomas told his father.

"Please, Thomas. Enlighten me."

"It's for the time on Chef Philippe's DVD. I think if we listen to it at this time, we will get a message from her. A message through Philippe."

Thomas retrieved the DVD from the metal box underneath his bed, and brought it downstairs. His father followed and sat at Helen's desk as Thomas inserted the DVD into her computer.

As the machine whirred to life, Thomas put his hand on his father's shoulder and leaned in.

She has something to tell us—to tell me!

Mr. Moran pressed the cursor until he reached the correct numbers on the time code. Then he pressed play and they listened as Philippe said:

Even if I can't be in the kitchen with you, you will still get an excellent result . . .

Chapter 43

Every year, his father asked Thomas to make a list of the things he wanted for his birthday. Because birthdays happened just once a year, it seemed important to ask for the right books, toys, and games since it would be months and months until Christmas and the opportunity to ask again.

Then of course there were all the things he wanted but could not ask for, such as for his mother to want to bake cookies. Or to play Ultimate Frisbee, like Aunt Sadie and Thomas had once seen a family doing when they drove past Grimmel Park on a Thursday afternoon. Now, with his mother gone almost four months, Thomas just wanted her.

The note was clear. But then again, the note had not spelled it out, as Aunt Sadie would say. There was still a shadow of doubt, which anyone who watched television knew meant that there was room for interpretation.

A little room left to imagine that she might come back.

Thomas thought about this as he lay wrapped inside her coat in UnderLand.

That evening, after dinner, Aunt Sadie, Mr. Walters, and Thomas's father sat at the table talking to Thomas about his birthday.

"Do you want to go somewhere?" Aunt Sadie asked Thomas. "Craig's Cruisers?"

"Or a restaurant?" his father asked.

In the past couple of years, just Martin was invited for dinner and cake. Because they never knew how Helen would feel. It was easier that way.

"Or," Mr. Walters said, "we could make a cake together."

"And go bowling," Thomas said. He'd been paying attention to happy people—or what he imagined happy people do. Every week the Morans got a penny-saver coupon book in the mail, and in it there was a full-page ad for a bowling alley called Richmond Lanes. The photo that went with the ad showed a mother and father and their two children. The son had just knocked down all the pins. The mother's hands were pressed to her face, her mouth forming an O of surprise. The father was shaking the son's hand and patting him on the back. The little sister was clapping.

Giselle could be the sister.

"I didn't know you liked bowling," Aunt Sadie said.

"I didn't either," Thomas said.

After Thomas had been sent to bed and Mr. Walters went home, Aunt Sadie stayed, talking with his father.

"I still don't understand why she went to that airport," his father said.

"Maybe she didn't either," Aunt Sadie replied.

"Maybe she was ready to go on a journey," Thomas said through the cold air register. "Like in my story."

"Thomas? I thought you were in bed. Have you heard this whole conversation?"

"I have very good hearing."

"Well I, for one, am glad we didn't find her message right away." Aunt Sadie spoke loud enough to include Thomas in the conversation. "I'm thinking . . . Helen didn't leave a note at home because she . . . she was hoping she'd find a way to come back."

There was a moment of silence as Thomas and Mr. Moran waited for Aunt Sadie to finish her thought.

"People have been so kind . . . all the food and coming out to search. Mrs. Sharp helping Thomas make that beautiful story that—"

"Aunt Sadie's got a boyfriend," Thomas said.

"Thomas! Well, anyway, now that you mention Jason, I do have an announcement to make. Will you come down, Thomas? It can't be comfortable lying with your cheek against the register all the time."

"What do you mean 'all the time'?" Mr. Moran said.

"Yes. *All* the time, Brian. Don't look at me like that. You can be so dense."

The next morning, Thomas sat at the kitchen table, separating the different languages of birds he could hear through the open window: chickadee, nuthatch, goldfinch. Mrs. Sharp was teaching him.

What was he doing this time last year on a Saturday at the end of March? What would he do in September when Aunt Sadie and Jason would be walking the Camino de Santiago?

For six weeks!

As he sat there, looking at Helen's teacups, which he'd brought out and arranged on the table, Thomas let thoughts of his mother wash over him—when she let him hold the hem of her dresses even when he was too old or let him drive his cars up her legs when he was supposed to be napping.

Was this what Reverend Amanda meant when she said that Helen lived on in our hearts, that this part of Helen—the memories—could fit anywhere—even into these teacups?

Rinsing his cereal bowl and placing it in the sink, Thomas went upstairs to get *The Big Book of Laughter and Happy Things* and some colored pencils. He'd never added anything to it but the one line. The book came at a time when laughter and happy things were like the dinosaurs—extinct. Now, back at the kitchen table, he opened the notebook to the first blank page and began to make a sketch. He drew one of Helen's flowered teacups and, since it was empty, he drew a butterfly on the rim, a tiny blue butterfly: a Karner blue.

Something about his mother's chair. Every time he came

into the kitchen, Thomas was reminded of her absence. But even sitting in that chair she'd been absent: silent and sad.

He didn't want to think about her that way anymore. As she had been. It wasn't all of her. She had been a little girl and a teenager and a mom, too. She'd been a happy mom for a long time.

First in his mind's eye and then on the page, Thomas drew their kitchen table out in the backyard. He made a hole in the center of it and placed the birdbath inside.

Then he drew Helen's chair and colored it green, with darker green vines twining up the legs and around the ladder back.

"What are you drawing?" his father asked. Thomas heard him at the sink. He smelled coffee and aftershave as Mr. Moran leaned over Thomas to inspect his drawing.

"Is that . . . our kitchen table and chair? In the backyard?"

"It's an art installation," Thomas told him.

"What do you know about art installations?"

"There's a Wikipedia page about them," Thomas told his father. "They're three-dimensional."

"What's that?" Mr. Moran asked, pointing to the middle of the table.

"The birdbath."

"You realize if you put the birdbath in the table, the birds will poop on it."

Thomas hadn't thought about that. He drew some poop. "It's part of life," he said.

"Are you saying you want to give our table to the birds?"

"I think we should put the table and her chair out there so she can be with the birds," Thomas said. "And the butterflies."

"So this...installation is for your mom?" Thomas's father sat down next to him. "I see your point about her wanting to be closer to the birds. But if we give our table to the birds, where will we eat?"

"We could get another one. Mr. Walters just got a workbench on craigslist for fifteen dollars."

"And these teacups of hers? Are they going out, too?"

Returning to his drawing, Thomas sketched half an orange into the sunflower teacup. "If you put an orange in like this"—he pointed with the tip of his pencil—"monarchs, painted ladies, gray hairstreaks...Mrs. Sharp knows all the butterflies that like fruit. A butterfly's mouth is like a straw; that's why they like juice so much."

"And for the ones that like nectar, do you want to plant flowers around the table?" his father asked. "Or is this installation meant to travel?"

"No. The legs are buried. It can't move. It's for Mom. Doesn't she always sit in her chair? Even if you can't see her?"

"Yes." Thomas's father pulled his chair next to Thomas's and sat down. "She does."

Thomas was still, thinking about the teacups. "But if we glue her teacups to the table, will they break when it freezes in the winter?"

"There's a special sealant you can paint on things you leave outdoors—to protect them," his father said.

Thomas nodded. "She should come in at night and go to bed."

"She does, Thomas," Mr. Moran said, putting his hand on Thomas's head. "She does."

Thomas regarded his father who was looking in the basket of magazines and catalogs by the kitchen door. They both knew what he had said was fanciful.

"May I . . . add to the project?" his father asked.

Thomas didn't say yes right away; he waited to see what his father would add.

Mr. Moran flipped through the pages of a gardening catalog and pointed to a photo of tall purple-blue flowers: "These are lupine, the main source of food supply for the Karner blue butterfly. Lupines like sandier soil than we have, so we'd have to build raised beds."

"But Mom said the Karner blue only lives up north. They won't come down here."

"I know. I've done my research. But after thinking about it, I decided that in my story they do, Thomas."

Thomas shrugged his shoulders.

Why couldn't he?

Returning to his drawing, Thomas drew the rest of their kitchen chairs and imagined guests into them. Everyone would visit: Mrs. Sharp and Martin and Giselle, even Mrs. Evans and Dave.

Both Daves!

But there would be no sadness. Adventures, yes. Danger,

lightning, high seas, maybe. But not sadness...only Happy Ever After.

Thomas consulted the photograph of the lupine flowers before he began sketching one coming out of the ground at Helen's feet. He couldn't be sure about the sadness for himself and his father and Aunt Sadie, but his imagination was very clear that there would be no more for his mother. She'd already had her share.

The moon and the fireflies and the night owls would visit, too.

And when they all went home, Thomas would come and sit with her for a while, to snuggle and gaze at the stars together, until it was time for him to go to bed.

Acknowledgments

So many people make a novel come alive. It is with a grateful heart that I thank the following individuals: Tad Caswell, for your search and rescue expertise; and Alyson Caillaud-Jones, for help with French. For special help in keeping track of many details, my brilliant young friends Sara Krahel and Emily Oxford. To my wonderful readers, Morgan Doane, Roger Gilles, Heidi Holst, Beth Leeson, Debbie McFalone, Amy Pence, Susan Roberts, Sarah Weber—discussing the story with you helped me to see it more clearly. Thank you!

Finally, thank you to my wonderful, insightful agent, Wendy Schmalz, who immediately thought of Margaret Ferguson for this manuscript. Margaret, thank you for your dedication to our vision of this book and for your devotion to stories that matter. Your thoughtful and wise commentary has immeasurably improved the story.

If you or someone you know is struggling, you are not alone. There are services and treatment options that may help. To find resources in your area, you can call the National Alliance on Mental Illness (NAMI) helpline at 1-800-950-6264